Where Is Olivia?

NANCY E. RYAN

PROLOGUE

As I finished reading Olivia's journals I could not hold back my tears. She was truly a remarkable woman.

Olivia Franklin, was a young, beautiful, British pediatric oncologist, who had been told her entire life that she was the mirror image of Princess Diana. In a chance encounter with Lt. Colonel Phillip Churchill at a fundraiser in London, a 30-year-old secret started to unravel when Churchill began to realize that this uncanny resemblance is no coincidence.

Secretly, on Christmas Eve 1980, Diana Spencer was forced to have her eggs harvested and fertilized with Prince Charles' sperm to prove her fertility before their engagement could be announced. After the embryos were confirmed as viable, the doctor was directed to destroy them but instead, he implanted one in his wife and destroyed the remainder. September 5, 1981, a biological daughter of Prince Charles and Princess Diana was born – Olivia Franklin – the year prior to Prince William's birth.

Olivia's journals unfold a frightening story of how Phillip Churchill under the direction of someone in Buckingham Palace made numerous attempts to kill her. Olivia was the rightful heir to the British throne after Prince Charles.

Pursued throughout Europe by Churchill, a man determined to eliminate her, Olivia found that she was embroiled in an international drama involving Scotland Yard, MI6, CIA, Interpol and Buckingham Palace.

Doctor Daniel Whittemore, Olivia's former lover, discovered Olivia's true identity. Recognizing the enormity of Olivia's situation, Daniel forced Olivia to flee London. Over the next year and a half Olivia wrote in her journals of her terrifying experiences the murder of her parents at the hands of Churchill and of how she fell back in love with Daniel.

Olivia disappeared abruptly leaving all her belongings and her journals in Africa. Where is Olivia?

Where Is Olivia?

NANCY E. RYAN

ACKNOWLEGEMENTS

Where Is Olivia? would not be possible without the help of my cousin Christine Adams and my friends Sue McCormick and Barbara DeSimone.

DEDICATION

This book is dedicated to all my girlfriends. Thank you for being in my life.

Chapter One

"Hold on!" Daniel shouted to Olivia as their Land Rover caught the edge of a deep rut in the dry dirt road. At 70 kilometers per hour, the car took quite a jolt as it raced southeast toward Bulawayo, the second largest city in Zimbabwe.

The two physicians were driving one of the safari trails that ran through Hwange National Park, the largest game preserve in the country. They had set out about an hour earlier after receiving a phone call from their friend, Chief Inspector Eddie Armstrong of Scotland Yard. Without explanation, he'd told them to drop everything and leave and go five miles east of Victoria Falls, and get to the city of Bulawayo—several hours' drive through the broad Savannah. But they knew Eddie well enough not to even question the situation and get out as fast as they could.

"What did Eddie say?" Olivia asked Daniel over the roar of the engine after they righted from yet another sharp turn.

"Not much," Daniel answered grimly. "Just that men were coming for us and that we had to move immediately."

"Men? What men?"

"The kind that tends to shoot at us."

Olivia's head slumped over into her hands. She'd thought they were finally done with all of that. She had been so excited by the grand opening of their little medical clinic, especially the celebration planned for the following Saturday at which her brothers, William and Harry, and Princess Kate would be in attendance. With Daniel's encouragement, Olivia had also extended the invitation to Charles, though no reply had ever been sent. She tried not to take that too personally—she supposed this was new and strange for all of them. Though they had known of Olivia's existence for some months now, she and her brothers had only met briefly, just as Olivia and Daniel were leaving for Africa. Ever since the violent events that had almost gotten her killed the previous April, the Royal Family had been trying to sort out the best way to ensure the safety of Charles's and Diana's oldest child. Apparently, something had gone awry.

"Why is this happening?" she shouted at the top of her lungs, though it was mostly lost in the din of the vehicle. She had been assured that the threat was eliminated and that the people who had tried to kill her were either dead or in jail.

But for some who were loyal to the crown, even in service to the Royal Family, Olivia was considered a threat. Should her existence become known to the world, the repercussions could be catastrophic. The way the public would react…many thought it was too much to risk, even to the point where members of the Royal Military Police—whose charter was to protect the Royal Family—had tried to kill her. Along the way, many others had been caught in the crossfire, including the couple that had raised her since birth. She had spent the past few months trying to disappear, but they had found her. Again.

Would this nightmare ever be over?

Just then, Daniel twisted the Land Rover into a sideways skid to avoid colliding with a herd of Cape buffalo that appeared out of nowhere over the crest of a hill. The car came to a sudden stop.

"Don't make any sudden moves," Daniel whispered.

Olivia understood the danger immediately. The buffalo were well used to vehicles passing through the area, but it still was far from wise to spook them.

"Whoa," Daniel hedged as a large bull brushed against the Land Rover, pushing it several feet.

Daniel put the car in reverse and slowly eased back. As he gazed at the track behind the vehicle, his face paled, "Shit!"

Olivia twisted to see a large dust plume off in the distance. "Is that a car?"

Without a word, Daniel shifted the Land Rover into low speed; turned down the hill that sloped from the road they'd been traveling, and maneuvered around the buffalo as quickly as he could.

Back up the slope and onto the safari track, he floored the accelerator, the wheels spinning furiously.

Driving faster now, Daniel veered off-road, pulled the vehicle behind some thick brush off to his right where they could hide until their pursuers passed. He cut the engine, and they sat in silence. Olivia waited, holding her breath.

A jeep carrying four men raced by on the road, disappearing out of sight.

"We better wait here for a while," Daniel said.

Olivia could hear the strain in his voice, and reached out to squeeze his hand. Then, without saying a word, she stepped from the Land Rover.

Finding a spot in the thicket where she could lie down on the ground and rest, Olivia stared at the deep blue African sky, wondering why this was happening to them yet again. The worst part was that she had dragged Daniel into all of this, too. He could never live a normal life, all because of her. Though he always assured her that this was what he wanted, she knew sometimes it wore on him, too.

A moment later, Daniel sat down beside her. "It's going to be okay. We'll make our way to Bulawayo and meet up with Eddie at the consulate."

Olivia released a deep breath. "And then what? We left the world as we knew it and took up residence in as remote a place as there is on the planet. Still, after only a few months, this is all happening again. Where do we go, Daniel? Where is it safe for us?"

Daniel said nothing, just reached out and took her hand.

They waited about a half hour before moving on. "Come on. We need to get going." Daniel helped Olivia to her feet and back into the Land Rover.

They drove at a moderate rate of speed for about another hour, constantly on the lookout for the men in the jeep. There was no sign of them.

"Maybe they were just sightseers," Olivia suggested.

Daniel said nothing. Either way, the potential for danger existed. Because if those *hadn't* been the men after them, then every second they spent dawdling meant that whoever was on their trail had more time to catch up to them.

About a half kilometer ahead, one of several man-made watering holes in the park had attracted a large number of impalas and zebras and a variety of native birds. As they pulled up to it, the engine spooked the impalas—thereby saving their lives as a pride of lions lunged from beneath the cover of trees.

Olivia stood, bracing herself against the side of the jeep to get a better view. "Did you see that?"

Almost immediately, four men emerged from another clump of trees, each armed with a rifle and sidearm.

Poachers was Olivia's first thought—until the men deliberately stepped into the path, blocking it, and aimed their rifles directly at them.

"Dismount the vehicle," commanded the solitary white man in the group in a British Rhodesian accent that was only heard among the native whites of this former crown colony. "Out, now!" He cocked his rifle.

Daniel and Olivia exited the car, slowly and carefully.

"Doctors Franklin and Whittemore, I presume," the Rhodesian said with a sly grin.

Daniel ever so slightly edged his way in front of Olivia. "What do you want?"

"Whatever I want, you can be sure I will have it."

Olivia swallowed. There was still a chance that this had nothing to do with her own past—that this was just a run-of-the-mill ambush. She decided to play that card as well as she could, raising her voice to its shrillest, most indignant tone. "You can't do this! We're subjects of the Crown, and known to be here by the British Embassy in Harare."

The Rhodesian spit on the ground and slung his rifle over his shoulder, squinting his eyes at the two of them. "Let me show you what I can do, Missy."

In less than two seconds, he had withdrawn his pistol and fired a single round into Daniel's right temple, killing him instantly.

Too shocked to move or speak, Olivia watched Daniel's body crumple to the ground. Daniel. Her Daniel. Then, screaming like a banshee, she lunged at the Rhodesian, knocking him to the dirt, causing him to lose his pistol as she pummeled him furiously.

Laughter erupted from the three black men, quite amused by the sight of this woman scratching, kicking, and punching their comrade. They did nothing to assist—the show was too uproarious.

Their laughter was punctuated by the sound of three simultaneous rifle shots, hitting each of the black men in the leg, shattering bone, ripping through muscle, and bringing them to the ground. Both Olivia and the Rhodesian immediately froze as three armed white men approached, disarming the thugs and pulling Olivia from the Rhodesian, who took a rifle butt to the jaw for his trouble.

Olivia raised her eyes in stunned disbelief, gaze catching on a familiar face. "Sir Paul," she murmured . . . just before slumping into his arms.

Chapter Two

In the sitting living room of a two-bedroom suite at the five-star Meikles Hotel in the capitol city of Harare, Zimbabwe, Sir Paul Richardson—former commissioner of the Metropolitan Police Service, Scotland Yard—sat with the two other men who had rescued Olivia and brought back the body of Dr. Daniel Whittemore. The two other men were Major Richard Ripley of the Royal Military Police, the Queen's Guard, and Inspector Nigel Prescott, still on active duty with Scotland Yard.

The three men sat around a table covered with files and classified documents.

In the larger of the two bedrooms, Olivia Franklin was fast asleep, heavily sedated after the trauma sustained earlier in the day. The poor thing had been virtually inconsolable, weeping and wailing Daniel's name. It was better that she have some time to recover while the rest of them figure out what their next move would be.

Sir Paul, well used to taking the lead in intelligence briefings, turned to Major Ripley. "So, let's run through what we have."

"The Crown still keeps a close eye on all the former colonies," Ripley informed him. "Zimbabwe has been visited by several Royals over the years, including Princess Diana in 1993. After a few plea bargain deals, we've confirmed that the white Rhodesian bloke is a petty criminal named Clive Ashby who was supposed to abduct Olivia and bring her to his employer, a mysterious figure named R.W. Curran."

"And what do we know of this Curran fellow?"

"Almost nothing until about an hour ago," Inspector Prescott spoke up. "But, pulling up his files from the Critical Response Wing of the Special Air Service, we've found that Curran joined the SAS in 1974 at the ripe old age of 19, that he was described in his intake assessment as being a man of 'great zeal.' "

"Hmmm." Sir Paul knew the type, and it hardly ever boded well. "What else?"

"Curran's first mission was in 1975—the Stansted hijacking. The SAS sent in a small unit from the CRW which overpowered the lone hijacker without firing a shot."

"I remember that," said Major Ripley. "A British Airways flight en route from Manchester to Heathrow was diverted to Stansted, where the Critical Response Wing showed the world why they are the best of the best when it comes to that sort of thing."

Prescott continued on. "A year later, his unit was deployed in force to Northern Ireland. In March of that year, Curran was credited with the abduction of suspected IRA Commander, Sean McKenna, whom he transported over the border. He received a commendation for that, and participated in several other successful high-risk missions in Ulster. Then, in April of '77, Seamus Harvey, another IRA leader was mysteriously assassinated; and while no one was ever named as the shooter, Curran was discharged from the service just a few weeks later.

"There's a hole there until 1981, when Curran went to work for Aegis Solutions, the private security firm."

"Aegis!" Ripley shook his head with thinly veiled disgust. "Calling them a security firm is like calling Special Forces a marching band."

"Indeed," Sir Paul agreed grimly. "What did he do for those cowboys?"

Prescott shook his head. "Unknown. All we know is that he spent the next fifteen years in the Middle East, and that he married a Palestinian woman whose name we don't have."

"And where is this Curran now?"

"We're not sure. We think he's based in London, but we've been unable to pinpoint his location. "

The conversation was interrupted by a knock at the door to the suite. Weapon drawn, Major Ripley moved to the door. "Who is it?"

"Housekeeping," came the distinctive voice of Chief Inspector Edward Armstrong, who'd been involved in the 'Princess Affair' since day one.

Ripley opened the door and was met by a broad grin.

"Hello, Richard. Put on a bit of weight, have you?"

Ripley said nothing, but glanced down at his belly, giving it a firm smack.

The grin faded from Eddie's face, and he sobered considerably. "So, how's our girl?"

"Asleep." Prescott nodded toward a closed bedroom door. "The hotel doctor gave her a strong sedative . . . she's been out for almost twelve hours. She was pretty ragged after..."

He hesitated, and the room fell silent, all eyes on Eddie. He and Daniel had been close friends—grown up together, gone to school together. He was the link that had gotten Eddie involved in Olivia's protection in the first place. And now...he was gone.

Ignoring their probing looks in his direction, Armstrong moved to the bedroom door and slipped inside, closing the door behind him.

"Eddie knows people at Aegis," Prescott said after a moment. "Former police and a few military. He may be able to get us more information on Curran."

Sir Paul sighed, deeply troubled by this new development. "If Aegis Solutions is involved, we're facing a formidable band of experienced professionals with considerable resources. Those guys are somewhere between the CIA and the Mafia, only a tad more ruthless."

Ripley shook his head, brooding. "But why would this Curran or anyone at Aegis be interested in Olivia? Was the goal abduction? After all, they could have put a bullet in Olivia's head too. Why and for whom and to what end?"

"It has to be someone with deep pockets," Prescott hypothesized. "Someone who knows Olivia's true identity and has an agenda that requires her physical presence."

"Someone with quite a bit of influence," Sir Paul agreed, "and nearly limitless resources. Someone…" He stopped himself short of saying what he had been thinking. Someone *royal*. After all, who else knew of Olivia's existence? And who else would have such a strong motive to track her down?

But Olivia had been so excited about meeting her new family. It was too terrible to think one of them could be behind this.

The men tossed around ideas for a few more minutes until Armstrong emerged from the bedroom.

"Eddie, we have a question for you," Sir Paul spoke up.

"Really?" returned Armstrong. "Because I have a question for you— where the hell is Olivia?"

Chapter Three

Olivia walked the broad ledge outside her Meikles hotel room window, negotiating her way to the corner about fifty feet away. There, against the windowless facade on the north side of the building, she braced herself before making the jump to a 90-foot Jacaranda tree, its electric purple blossoms almost blinding in the midday sun.

Olivia had always been athletic, and the climb down to the street brought back memories of her childhood when she used to sneak out of her parents' house in Knightsbridge to meet friends. This climb was even simpler, as the brilliant old tree provided large, strong limbs for her descent. On her person she carried two passports—one in the name of Olivia Franklin, another Melissa Spencer; a letter from Armstrong; one pre-paid credit card for Melissa Spencer; a cashier's check in dollars drawn on a Barclays account in London, also made out to Melissa Spencer; and $2,000 American dollars. All were safely stowed in one of the deep pockets of her cargo shorts. Olivia had given Eddie 250,000 pounds for safekeeping before leaving for Africa, a decision she is so bloody thankful for today.

Olivia hit the ground running.

Seconds later, she flagged down a taxi.

As the taxi wound through the congested streets of Harare, Olivia could not shake the image of Daniel being gunned down. The whole universe had been turned upside-down in a matter of seconds. She still couldn't comprehend it fully, only ached inside like nothing she had ever experienced before. Even the death of her parents almost a year ago, as horrible as that was, was nothing like this.

The tears threatened to overwhelm her yet again, but she pulled herself together. Daniel would have wanted her to survive. She had to be strong.

"Thank you," she said to the driver as he pulled up to the curb of the international terminal at the airport.

Inside, she looked up at the large information display and made a mad dash to the Air Zimbabwe counter, where she purchased a ticket for a flight to Johannesburg that had already started boarding.

Taking her seat on the short-hop commuter flight to South Africa's largest city, she closed her eyes and tried to settle her nerves.

She was back in the Great Ormond Street Hospital recuperating from day surgery. It was June 3, 1991 and Olivia was almost 10. She'd always had ears that stuck out and was so self-conscious about it that she finally convinced her parents, Arthur and Elizabeth Franklin, to let her have surgery to pin them back. It was minor surgery and no big deal from a medical standpoint, but to Olivia it meant everything.

 That afternoon as Olivia exited the hospital, she looked up to see her idol, Princess Diana, hurrying in. Prince William had been rushed to the hospital with a skull fracture, the result of a fellow student accidently hitting him in the head with a golf club. Olivia stared at the beautiful, blond apparition rushing by, her face frantic with worry.

Olivia turned to tell her parents what she'd just seen—when they suddenly exploded into fireballs, consumed in leaping, roaring flames.

Opening her mouth to scream, Olivia suddenly leapt forward in time, back to yet another memory. Now, it was June 12, 1995, and 13-year-old Olivia was in her ballet class. The princess had visited the class that day and singled out Olivia from all the other ballerinas, calling her a mirror reflection of herself at that age. It was a moment that Olivia would never forget. The princess was so beautiful, and talked to her for almost five minutes.

All the while, her own parents watched in from the window, mouths opened in soundless screams as the flames continued to lick at their flesh. In the background, a gunshot cracked through the air.

" . . . and place your seatbacks and tray tables in the upright position," said a voice over the intercom, jolting Olivia from her sleep. She took in a few breaths, steadying herself, as she wiped away tears running down her cheeks.

The main concourse of the international terminal at O.R. Tambo International Airport in Johannesburg had many shopping options. Olivia bought a small travel bag, a couple of silk scarves to cover her hair, a novel to distract her on the long flight to Dubai, a new leather bound journal and a pair of sunglasses to cover her swollen tear-filled eyes.

In the bathroom, she took out her $100,000 cashier's check and stuffed it into her bra. A check for that amount was liable to attract the attention of a customs official, and that she didn't need.

She would fly out on Air Emirates, connecting in Dubai to a flight for Los Angeles. It would be a long twenty-four hours, but necessary to make a clean getaway.

Or so she hoped.

"Yes. Yes, I understand. Oh, by the way, you can kiss the rest of your money goodbye, you wanker."

R.W. Curran switched off his cell phone and slammed it on the desk. He leaned forward on one hand, using the other to run fingers through his short, cropped hair. He'd been warned that Olivia Franklin was alarmingly resourceful, but this was getting ridiculous. So far he'd found a signal for her laptop in a hotel room in Harare, but by the time any of his people had gotten to the scene, she was long gone. Now the best he could do was issue a **BOLO** on her and sit back and wait. He somehow doubted his employer would be very happy to hear that.

Almost immediately, his mobile phone rang again. Thinking it was a callback from his previous conversation, he flushed with rage, ready to spew out a slew of curse words—until he saw the conspicuously unmarked number and quickly answered it.

"Curran here." He took in a deep breath, steadying himself, wiping his slick palms on his trousers to keep from dropping his phone. "Just a minor setback . . . No, I've got it under control. I'm expecting a full report from my people later today . . . Yes, I'll get right back to you—Your Majesty."

At the Meikles Hotel in Harare, Eddie Armstrong, Sir Paul, Prescott, and Ripley searched Olivia's room for any clues she might have inadvertently left behind in her escape.

"It's clear she went out the window," Sir Paul surmised. "The only other exit is through that door to the sitting room, and there have never been fewer than two of us in there since we got here."

Major Ripley shook his head. "But why? And why leave her computer and phone behind?"

"Perhaps she was abducted," Prescott suggested.

"I don't think so." Eddie walked to the window, opening it up and climbing onto the ledge. "If she was unconscious, it would take at least two men—one to lift her up and hand her to the other out on the ledge. I don't think there's enough room up here for a man, however strong and agile, to carry a 5'10" woman along this ledge."

"And even if he could," Richardson piped up, "how does he get her down three stories to the street?"

"So let's say she was conscious, with a gun stuck in her ribs—do as we say or you're dead."

"No way." Armstrong climbed back into the room. "It's an empty threat. If they wanted her dead, she'd be dead already. Olivia would have known that, called their bluff."

Sir Paul released a frustrated breath, slamming his palm against the wall. "It just doesn't make any sense. Why would she try to get away from us? Why leave her computer and phone? The only thing missing is her passport. She even left her wallet behind."

Eddie stepped in closer, clapping an encouraging hand on his shoulder. "Well, a passport only has one real purpose. My money's on the airport. What do you say we drop by, see if anyone's spotted a gorgeous blonde hopping on a plane?"

Chapter Four

Olivia shifted uneasily in seat 4A, waiting until the plane was about half full. Then, when the time was right, she abruptly grabbed her carry-on bag and hurried to the door where passengers were streaming in.

"I forgot my computer!" she called to the confused flight attendant as she blew past her and ran down the jet-way. "My computer!" she shouted again, running past another attendant collecting boarding passes at the gate.

As she rounded a corner in the terminal concourse, Olivia slowed to a walk so as not to draw attention to herself. Moments later she approached the desk at Gate F, making a plaintive face at the man behind it. "Please tell me you have a seat left. The company I work for just wrecked my entire week."

The mildly surprised flight supervisor tapped on his computer for a couple of seconds. "I'm afraid all we have left is a first-class seat."

She reached for her credit card. "I'll take it."

He furrowed his brow at her. "Miss, that ticket is $3700 USD."

"Good!" she exclaimed with exaggerated outrage. "The company is going to pay through the nose for this."

Grinning conspiratorially back at her, the attendant tapped a few more keys on his computer. "One first-class ticket to Atlanta, Georgia…"

R.W. Curran's mood had improved considerably since one of his tech experts at Aegis had been able to track Olivia; she was on a plane to Dubai. He had men there whohe could count on to meet her flight and detain her until he could get there; and he was looking forward to telling his employer that things were back on track.

Curran rose from his desk chair and moved to a cabinet on the far wall of his office, where he removed a glass and a bottle of Glenlivet 25 year single malt whisky. Returning to his desk, he poured himself two fingers, promptly threw it down, and slammed the glass on his desk. Picking up the phone with his left hand while pouring another shot with his right, he punched in the number of his employer.

"Yes?" came the voice at the other end.

"Good news," said Curran. "We have reacquired the subject, who is on a flight to Los Angeles with a stopover in Dubai. My men will meet her in the desert, by which time I will be well on my way to the Sheikhdom."

"Good. The sooner this is taken care of, the better."

"Yes, Your Highness, I understand."

"Oh, and Curran? I would appreciate it if in the future you choose your words more carefully. I don't know how they do things in the SAS, but in the navy, 'reacquired' means she's either shackled to your wrist or sleeping comfortably in your duffle bag."

The phone went dead, and Richard W. Curran took a healthy swig of Glenlivet.

The plane hadn't even left the gate when the Delta flight attendants began to approach, offering first-class passengers champagne and other libations.

"No, thank you," said Olivia. "Perhaps later." *When this plane is in the air.*

There was no one in the seat next to her, and she quietly said a prayer of gratitude. Hours upon hours of idle chitchat or a snooping neighbor were the last things she could handle at that instant.

Olivia got up to retrieve some items from her carry-on bag in the overhead compartment, then sat back down with the paperback novel and journal she had purchased at the airport—along with the envelope Armstrong had given her.

Sitting back, she closed her eyes and recalled the fleeting encounter she'd had with him at the hotel.

Olivia was just waking up when Eddie entered the room with his right index finger pressed to his lips. She didn't stir or make a sound, just watched as he took some items from his pocket, grabbed her passport, and removed the wallet with her credit cards. Then he opened the window and gestured to her to come over.

"Are you alert enough to go for a little walk?"

Olivia nodded that she was.

"Good. The ledge is wide and the corner of the building is only about twenty feet. Go left around the corner, where you'll find a tree to easily climb down."

Olivia shoved her passports and letter into the deep pockets of her cargo shorts, looked at the broad ledge, and without hesitation climbed through the window. She had learned months ago that when Armstrong said 'duck,' you hit the ground without thinking.

Now, on the plane, Olivia opened her eyes, fastened her seatbelt, and removed a letter from the envelope. She had already read it three times.

Olivia,

I'm afraid that despite my best efforts, you're once again in mortal danger. I believe a mercenary named R.W. Curran has been hired to abduct you. And though I don't have the evidence yet I need to prove it one way or the other, I have reason to believe he was hired by someone from the royal family, which means you're in more danger than you've ever been in before.

You have to disappear, with no assistance from anyone who has helped you in the past. No one, not even me, can be contacted. Disappear without a trace. Do not call, email, or in any way contact anyone you know. I want you to go to Palm Beach, Florida. I have arranged for you to stay with my late sister Julia's husband, John Bradford Verner. John has agreed to give you safe coverage. He has a 7-year-old son Miles, my nephew, and you will be Miles's governess. John is unaware of your true identity. He is expecting to house Melissa Spenser, no questions asked. John thinks you are in hiding from a well-connected abusive husband. I trust John with my life and now with yours.

I will contact you by Post, at John's address, 200 South Ocean Boulevard, Palm Beach.

Additionally, I will go to Zimbabwe to retrieve your personal belongings and find your journals.

All the best,

Eddie

Finishing the letter, Olivia sighed and leaned back in her seat. She had no idea where she was headed or if Eddie's brother-in-law would even be able to protect her, but if there was anyone she trusted in the entire world, it was Eddie. Eddie was Daniel's closest chum and now Olivia's closest friend/brother. Olivia prayed that Eddie would find her journals.

The journals documented her time with Daniel.

As the flight prepared for takeoff, Olivia tried to distract herself with her novel, but neither could hold her interest—her mind was too restless. Instead, she took one of the free newspapers that the attendants were passing out to the first-class passengers, skimming through the headlines until one stuck out at her. Olivia's jaw literally fell open.

British Monarchy Scraps Rule of Male Succession in New Step to Modernization

By John F. Burns

Published: October 28, 2011

LONDON — The 16 countries that recognize the British monarch as head of state struck a historic blow for women's rights on Friday, abolishing male precedence in the order of succession to the throne. But the possibility of a Catholic monarch will have to wait, nearly 500 years after Henry VIII broke with Rome.

The decision to overturn the centuries-old tradition known as primogeniture was accompanied by the scrapping of a constitutional prohibition on the monarch's marrying a Roman Catholic. But the rule that reserves the throne to Protestants will remain.

The changes will have no immediate impact on the existing line of succession. The current heir to the throne, Prince Charles, will retain that position, and is in any case the oldest child of his parents, Queen Elizabeth II and Prince Philip. The second in line to the throne is his firstborn child, Prince William . . .

Olivia put down the paper, pressing her eyes shut. It was all starting to make sense now. The pieces of why she had suddenly become the focus of a Royal Conspiracy yet again suddenly began to fit together. Because despite popular belief, Prince William wasn't Charles's firstborn.

I am now first in line after Charles, she realized.

And someone wanted to kill her for it.

But she would give them a real chase, first.

Olivia's plane landed thirty-five minutes late due to severe thunderstorms in the Atlanta area, but she was pretty confident that no one would be greeting her at the gate. As she expected, she blew through Passport Control without incident, the $100,000 check she was carrying, safe from scrutiny.

Mindlessly, she followed the flow of passengers from Customs to Baggage Claim, despite the fact that she had no checked baggage, just a small carry-on bag. Once there, she was greeted by the sight of limo drivers holding cardboard signs with the names of various passengers.

Why not? She asked herself, spotting a chauffeur holding a sign reading *Ms. Simpson.*

"Hello, you must be my driver."

"Barbara Simpson?"

"Please," she answered with her most charming grin, "call me Barb."

The driver had seemed a bit taken aback when she'd requested he take her to Augusta, Georgia—a two-and a half hour trip, and that didn't include the travel time back—but quickly agreed once Olivia dropped hints about a very generous tip.

As they approached the city of Augusta, Olivia leaned forward. "Just drop me at the Marriott, please." Olivia almost whispered, " Two Tenth Street."

A few minutes later they were in front of the hotel, where she handed the driver $500. "I assume this will cover it."

"Thank you, Barb. That's very generous. Have a good stay."

Minutes later, Olivia was inside the hotel, looking for the Concierge Desk. "May I help you?" asked an attractive woman behind the desk.

"Could I borrow your phone book for a couple of minutes?"

"Absolutely," answered the woman with her best Marriott smile. "Is there something I can look up for you?"

"I'm not quite sure of the name." Olivia reached for the book. "It'll only be a minute."

It was actually less than a minute before Olivia found what she was looking for. After returning the book, Olivia went back outside and approached a young parking attendant. "Excuse me. Can you tell me where Greene Street is?"

"About three blocks that way," he said pointing. "Can I call you a cab?"

She flashed him a warm but frazzled smile. "You know, I've been cramped up on an airplane for hours, and it's such a beautiful day, I think I'll stretch my legs. Thanks anyway."

About 30 minutes later, Olivia reached 1128 Greene Street.

"It's about ten hours from here including rest stops," said the man behind the Greyhound ticket counter. "The next bus for West Palm leaves at 3:05PM arrives in West Palm Beach at 9:40AM."

"Excellent," said Olivia, opening her purse.

She paid the man, took a nearby seat in the waiting area, and pulled out her new journal. As she began her entries her eyes filled up, but she knew she needed to put her feelings down on paper.

Olivia's bus pulled into the Greyhound station on Tamarind Avenue in West Palm Beach, Florida where she thanked the driver and exited the motor coach. It felt good to stretch her legs after so many hours of being cooped up on planes and seventeen hours on a bus.

After a few minutes of looking around, gathering maps and bus schedules, Olivia realized she couldn't be in a better place to continue her mad dash to obscurity. Tamarind Avenue is the city's central hub for Greyhound, Amtrak, the Tri-rail commuter train which serves much of South Florida, and for the county's Palm-Tran bus system which has routes along every major thoroughfare from the beach to the western suburbs and from north to south. It is also the easiest place in the city to get a taxi.

Since it was her plan to use none of the above, it was likely that anyone who might be trying to follow her trail would hit a dead end right here.

Glancing at a street map of the downtown area, she decided to take the twenty- minute walk to the West Palm Beach Public Library—a good place to access the Internet and plan her next steps.

The weather in the city was typically glorious for a late October day. Temperatures in the high 70s had replaced the oppressive heat of summer with low humidity under blue sun-filled skies. Olivia was pleased to get a bit of exercise and take in the surroundings. As she skirted the edge of City Place, the newly constructed downtown retail and high-rise condo community, the number of signs advertising vacancies for both apartments and store space struck her. The Great Recession of 2008 to 2011 had not been kind to those who had built just prior to the housing crash. Indeed, most of downtown West Palm Beach was completed just before the bottom dropped out of the real estate market. Famished, Olivia decided to find a Starbucks. Olivia needed a great cup of tea and she knew that Starbucks had Tazo Tea and decent scones.

Leaving the Starbucks, Olivia headed west on Clematis Street; Olivia entered the newly completed public library, around the corner from the newly completed courthouse and the newly completed City Hall, and all the newly completed empty shops. She followed the signs inside the library to the public computer area, and without so much as showing a library card, logged on to the Internet.

As her fingers hovered above the keyboard, Olivia suddenly panicked.

"Who's out there?" she whispered. "Police organizations, intelligence agencies, the military?

"Who's killing us—my parents and Daniel and the good men who've tried to protect us? Who's pulling the strings in this bizarre Elizabethan tragedy?"

Eddie had said in his letter that he believed it was a member of the royal family. Olivia didn't want to believe it could be true, especially not with the budding relationship she was beginning to form with William and Harry. Besides, she had renounced the title, the position—all she wanted was a relationship with her brothers. So why would someone want her to die for that?

With a flurry of fingers tapping keys on the computer before her, Olivia restricted her research to general information about local banks.

After making several phone calls from the pay phone at the library, Olivia walked back on to Clematis Street and into a walk-in hair salon. One hour later Olivia was a brunette with a short hairstyle. Directly across the street Olivia found a very trendy eyewear shop. Olivia emerged from the store. Gone were her beautiful blue eyes, she was now a brown-eyed beauty. Melissa Spencer was born.

Six blocks to Okeechobee Boulevard where she caught the eastbound bus toward Royal Palm Beach. Exiting the bus at Haverhill Boulevard she walked a half block to the Bank Atlantic branch at 5737 Okeechobee.

Looking very upper crust and self-assured, she took a seat in the waiting area, indicating that she was there for something other than the typical business that a teller would handle.

"Can I help you?" said a pretty young woman wearing a nameplate that said *Betty Jo.*

"Hi. I believe we spoke on the phone earlier. I'm Melissa Spencer," she said, extending her hand.

"Yes, Ms. Spencer. It's nice to meet you. I'm Betty Jo Gordon"

"Please call me Melissa," she responded with a bright smile. The two of them proceeded to Betty Jo's office behind a wall of glass.

Removing the certified check for $100,000 from her purse, Olivia placed it on the desk as Betty Jo pulled out the forms to open a new account.

Having spoken with the managers of several local banks, Olivia selected Bank Atlantic for two particular reasons: they were one of the few banks in the area that was open seven days a week, which could come in handy if she ever had to withdraw her funds on short notice; and Bank Atlantic had a service that was not offered by any other bank Olivia had ever heard of. They had a machine on the premises that allowed them to manufacture debit cards in two or three minutes rather than the seven to ten days it normally takes to get one.

Olivia answered several questions about the type of account she wanted to open and within fifteen minutes she left the bank with a Gold Debit MasterCard, which because it was not a credit card did not require a credit check that might set off alarms that the techno-creeps would notice.

Crossing the wide boulevard, Olivia took the eastbound bus on Okeechobee heading back toward downtown. At the 1000 block of Okeechobee, she got off the bus, crossed the street, and walked to the entrance of the Marriott Hotel, where she asked the doorman to call her a taxi.

"Where to?" asked the driver. Olivia took a scrap of paper from her pocket and read the address to the driver.

"200 South Ocean Blvd . . . Palm Beach Island."

"Time to meet Mr. John Bradford Verner & son," Olivia said to herself.

"What do you mean, you lost her trail?" growled the usually polished, well-educated voice on the other end of the line.

R.W. Curran flinched, running a hand over his face. "*Temporarily.* Only temporarily. She proved to me more resourceful than I anticipated—good genes, I suppose."

The words, meant to be flattering and appeasing, fell flat. "I was told you were the man for the job, Curran. I would hate to be disappointed, but if you can't manage, I will find someone to take your place."

Hearing the threat in the words, Curran swallowed, hard. Not only would his employer find someone to finish the job with Olivia, but he'd find someone to take care of Curran, too. There couldn't be too many witnesses, after all.

"I understand, Your Highness. I won't fail you again."

"See that you don't." On his end of the line, Curran's employer furiously pressed the power button on his secure mobile phone, ending the call.

Someone rapped tentatively on his office door. "Darling? Is everything all right in there? I heard shouting."

"Fine," he barked back hoarsely, then took a moment to clear his throat and manage his voice. "Fine, darling. Just a mild problem, but it's been dealt with now."

Another pause, which meant he hadn't been entirely convincing, but she would let it pass for now. "Well, hurry along then. We'll be late to the outing with the Middletons."

"One moment. I'll be right there."

Waiting to make certain she'd left the door, the employer fished a key from his pocket and opened the secret panel on the underside of his desk. From there, he fished out two photographs—one of Diana, the other of Olivia. Holding them side by side, they were nearly identical, save be a few slight differences.

"Damn you," he seethed quietly, and it was unclear, even to him, to which one he was referring. Both of them, perhaps. Diana, Olivia—it was all the same.

She would never let him be.

Rising to his feet, he threw both into the fire and watched with no little satisfaction as they burned.

Two Months Later

Chapter Five

Olivia's heart raced in her chest as she ran, barefoot, along the sandy beach, her pursuer rapidly closing in behind her. It was only a matter of time before he caught her; still, she propelled herself forward, not willing to give up that easily. The stairs leading up to the back of the mammoth, sprawling beach house on Ocean Boulevard loomed before her. In a matter of minutes, she would reach them, be on her way to safety—

A heavy weight barreled into the backs of her knees, tackling her down into the sand. She screamed in protest—the sound quickly dissolving into laughter as small fingers found the bottoms of her feet and the insides of her armpits. "Miles, stop!" she howled through her giggles, squirming to be free of him.

An impish face came into view, darkened by the brightness of the sun behind him, highlighting the few streaks of blond in his curls. "Say you surrender!" he demanded, even as he launched a fresh attack on her ribcage.

Gasping now for breath, Olivia obediently raised her hands. "I surrender! I surrender."

Miles waited for her to catch her breath again before falling down into the sand beside her. A hesitant moment later, his curly head managed to find its way to the crook of her shoulder, resting there. "Melissa? You're my best friend."

Tears filled Olivia's eyes that had nothing to do with her laughter now. Almost three months before, Eddie had sent her to this address— home of one John Bradford Verner, his billionaire brother-in-law— claiming that he would provide her with all the credentials she would need to fill in the position as governess to Verner's seven-year-old son, Miles. At the time, she had protested violently, much to Eddie's evident surprise.

"What's the problem, Franklin?" he'd teased with an attempt at his usual sparkle, though much of that seemed to have left him since Daniel's murder. "I thought you liked kids."

"I do," Olivia had agreed darkly, "but we both know what happens to the people around me."

Still, Eddie had been insistent that she at least meet the family, and there wasn't much she could deny him after everything he'd done for her and Daniel. She'd resolved herself to take one look at the fancy house and the snooty billionaire and his spoiled kid, just to appease Eddie, then find the quickest bus to New Mexico and never look back. But one meeting with Miles had been enough to change all that.

He was playing by himself in the sand the first time she saw him, a spade and bucket at his side as he dug furiously into the ground, the gigantic mansion looming behind him. At Olivia's approach, he glanced up, squinting at her against the sun. "Who are you?"

"Melissa," Olivia had returned simply. It was the name of a girl Eddie had gone to school with ages ago, and one he'd hoped his old girlfriend wouldn't mind him borrowing.

Miles smiled at Melissa, giggling at her English accent. He motioned her closer. "Wanna see my special secrets?"

Olivia ventured forward to peer into the hole Miles had been work- ing so hard on. Inside were dozens upon dozens of seashells, not two alike but each one more beautiful then the next. He beamed up proudly at her, tongue poking out through one of his missing front teeth. "Mom and I used to look for shells together. Janett says every time I find one now, it means my mom is thinking about me."

Swallowing back the lump in her throat, Olivia glanced down at the collection he must have gathered carefully and painstakingly, the only connection to his lost mother. "Well," she said when she was finally able, "look how much she loved you."

Against her better judgment, she'd asked Eddie for the full story. Eddie had established a secure email for Olivia and his responding e-mail had been terse and to the point, but had nonetheless conveyed the horror of that fateful day: on 17 March, 2009, Julia Armstrong Verner—Miles's mother and Eddie's sister—had been on a boating trip with some friends, snorkeling in the Intracoastal. A driver of an approaching boat who'd had one too many drinks crashed into the boat, throwing then 4-year-old Miles into the water. Fortunately, he'd been wearing a life vest, but Julia had not fared so well when the drunk drove his boat over the area where she was snorkeling, nearly decapitating her.

The story was horrific on multiple levels; but the image Olivia could not quite erase from her mind was the little boy, adrift in the water, screaming for a mother who would never again come to his rescue. And despite her better judgment, she'd known then that she could not leave him.

Now, lying beside him on the sun-warmed sand, Olivia took a second to press her eyes shut, composing herself, before responding, "You're my best friend, too, Miles."

But it was a beautiful day, and the boy was seven, no time for any lingering sentimentality. He was already on his feet, doing cartwheels and demanding Olivia's attention. "Watch this, Melissa! Look at me!"

A shadowed figure appeared at the top of the steps leading up to the beach house—Janett, the live-in housekeeper. "Melissa!" called the middle-aged woman, cupping her hands over her mouth. "There's someone here to see you."

The words sent a shiver of panic through Olivia's gut, instantly darkening the once-bright day. The only person who knew she was here was Eddie, and surely he would have called ahead.

"All right!" Olivia called back, trying to infuse her voice with as much cheerfulness as possible. "Can you keep an eye on Miles briefly please?

But Miles had chosen this inopportune time to become uncharacteristically clingy. "I want to come, too!" He clutched at Olivia's arm, half-hanging off her. "Take me with you, Melissa. I want to see who's at the door."

A brief, terrible image imprinted itself in Olivia's mind—answering the door to realize it was one of the men chasing her. Miles running out to greet them with his usual cacophony of questions—only to be met with a bullet to the skull.

Just like Daniel.

Shuddering, Olivia did her best to detangle herself from him. "It will be much more fun to stay down here and show Janett your gymnastics."

"No, I'm bored. I want to come inside—"

"Miles, you're being very naughty right now!" Olivia snapped at him finally, jerking free of his grasp. "You'll stay down here and play with Janett, and I don't want to hear anything more about it."

The blood pounding in her ears managed to drown out most of the shocked, sullen silence, though it did not erase the memory of tears springing to Miles's eyes as he turned his back to her. She began the long climb to the top of the stairs, meeting Janett's gaze briefly and seeing the other woman's surprise before she managed to blink it away. It was not like her to be so cross; she would apologize later, if there were a later.

Don't come upstairs if you hear gunshots, she wanted to warn the other woman. *Take Miles and run as fast as you can.*

But the words died in her throat, impossible to say aloud.

Finally, Olivia was in the house, approaching the front door. Through the huge bay windows, she caught a brief glimpse of the man waiting on the other side. His back was turned toward her, his hair buzzed close to the head, and he wore blue jeans and a Rolling Stones worn-out tee shirt. The portions of his arms that were visible were covered with angry tattoos. His stance was the kind she had come to associate with law-enforcement agents on both sides of the pond. Not Eddie Armstrong, though he looked somehow strangely familiar all the same.

With trembling hands, Olivia opened the door. "Can I help you?"

The man turned, catching her with a broad, familiar smile. "Hey, Princess. Heard you were in a bit of a pickle."

Chapter Six

Friday September 5, 1997

"And then I told her, that's not a banana." Arthur Franklin paused, waiting for a reaction from his wife and daughter. "Get it? It's not a banana."

Fresh off a six-hour flight from London, Elizabeth Franklin managed a wan smile for her husband's benefit. "Yes, dear. Very funny."

16-year-old Olivia bit back her own smile at the exchange, pretending to be absorbed with the scenery, which was not difficult to do. It was her first time in Boston, and she was amazed at the bigness and brightness of the city, so unlike anything in England. Undoubtedly the Americans all marveled at how old and historic it was with its beautiful architecture, but all she saw was its newness—the lights and gleaming silver structures.

"…People at the office think I'm a hoot," Arthur was grumbling from the front seat of the shuttle to their hotel.

"Darling, I smiled. You just couldn't see me since you were facing the other direction."

"Well, so long as you laugh <u>out loud</u> during the actual speech tomorrow. Nothing more odious than a fertility conference with no mildly inappropriate humor to liven things up."

In the backseat, Olivia and her mother exchanged a conspiratorial glance. Elizabeth took Olivia's hand, giving a bracing smile. "Actually, darling, we were thinking we'd opt out of the conference, go have a bit of a look-around the city."

Arthur spluttered with indignation, swiveling around to face them. "Miss my conference, so you can ride a bloody tour bus and buy some garish souvenirs?"

"So we can see Boston," Elizabeth corrected him, "which will be your only daughter's first and perhaps only time in this city. Besides which, I think we could all do with a bit of cheering up."

Her tone was light, but Olivia heard the meaning underneath. The whole country had been despondent ever since Princess Diana's tragic death only days before, but for some reason it seemed to have stricken Olivia particularly hard. She'd found herself almost constantly on the verge of tears, empty and hollow and sad, as if something important and irretrievable had been snuffed out inside of her.

She expected Arthur to come back with some gruff retort about snapping out of it—he'd never been one for sentimentality, and his teenage daughter's unpredictable moods and shifting hormones seemed to be a source of constant irritation—but instead he fell silent, the line of his shoulders visibly tensing. "Well," he said finally after a long moment's pause, "I suppose Boston is a once-in-a-lifetime experience."

Elizabeth exchanged a conspiratorial, victorious smile with her daughter, which Olivia did her best to return, though she couldn't help but wonder at her father's abrupt shift in mood at the reference to Princess Diana's death. Perhaps he was more broken up about it than he let on.

After checking in at the Ritz Carlton on Arlington Street, the Franklin family made their way to the bar to grab a bite to eat. The flight had eaten away most of their day, but the cramped quarters and terrible plane food had done nothing to suppress their appetites.

The Ritz was a beautiful hotel, and though not as gorgeous as the one in London, nothing could quite rival the view of the Boston Public Gardens from inside the beautiful, sophisticated bar. Olivia almost found herself caught up in the beauty and romance of it all—until she overheard snippets of conversation from the tables around her. Almost all were about the recent deaths of Diana and Mother Teresa, and very few were flattering.

"...All this commotion over the death of some castoff princess, completely over-shadowing the death of a philanthropist who devoted her life to helping others," spoke up a particularly loud man at the bar.

Olivia felt tears flood her eyes at the insinuation. Of course the death of Mother Teresa was a terrible loss to the world at large, but why did that have to make Princess Diana's death anything less tragic?

"Guess you must have missed the point of Mother Teresa's message then," spoke up another voice from across the room in response. *"Because her life's goal was to show that we're all important, whether you happen to be a beggar on the streets, a child born with AIDS, or a 'castoff princess'—who, by the way, devoted a pretty good chunk of her life to helping others, too."*

Olivia swiveled in her seat to see who had spoken. To her surprise, it was a boy who looked only to be a year or two older than her, surprisingly well spoken for someone his age. He was lean and looked to be average-sized, with light brown hair, pale green eyes, and an interesting if not overly handsome face. Two older people sat with him—presumably his mother and father—and across from him sat his own mirror image of a brother, almost down to the last freckle.

Catching his gaze, Olivia offered a smile of gratitude, which was returned with a nod of acknowledgment. His brother turned to see what had caught his attention—and stared, squinting at Olivia, before his expression dissolved into a confused frown.

Before Olivia could piece together what had happened, her father was crossing the room to shake hands with the twins and their parents. "Well said." Arthur's enthusiastic voice rang through the bar, effectively silencing all other remarks on the subject. "Couldn't have put it better, myself."

Ever the spokesman, Arthur was quick to make friends at the table, and soon the two families were joining together to eat their meal. Elizabeth and Arthur became engrossed in conversation with Doris and Bill Connors, leaving Olivia to entertain the two boys. She quickly learned that Fred was the name of the one who had spoken up in defense of Diana, and that his twin's name was Luke.

"Freddie here can't help but stick up for the lowly and downtrodden," Luke said, clasping his arm around his brother's shoulder with obvious affection. *"He's going to be studying criminal law at Northeastern University. Hence, the super-man complex."*

Fred just laughed good-naturedly at the ribbing. "And Luke here is going into broadcast journalism at Emerson, which is why he's knee-deep in pretty much every tabloid, newspaper, and magazine available north of the Mason-Dixon line."

Olivia followed his sweeping gesture, confirming that there was, in fact, quite an impressive stack at Luke's side. "All right then," she bantered back, feeling instantly at ease with these two happy, carefree young men, "fill me in. Who's having Elvis's baby this week?"

"Marilyn Monroe," Luke quipped back without missing a beat, before pulling up the nearest newspaper—a <u>Boston Globe</u>. "Actually, the big story of the hour is—surprise, surprise—Diana and Mother Teresa." He glanced down at one of the photographic images of Diana before holding it up to Olivia's inspection. "Anyone ever tell you that you look uncannily like her?"

Olivia stared back at the picture, a bit taken aback. She'd always sort of hoped so, had maybe caught a familiar expression or feature in the mirror, but she'd assumed that was wishful thinking. Didn't every girl want to be Princess Diana?

"Are you only saying that because I'm British?" she teased back. "That's a bit racist, I think."

"You're British?" Fred joked, feigning amazement. "I thought you were from Tennessee."

Luke spoke over his brother, almost on top of him, "And besides, it wouldn't be racist, it would be…I don't know, nationalist?"

Olivia laughed along with them. It felt good to laugh again, to really laugh. It didn't get rid of the sadness inside entirely, but it made it easier somehow.

Fred took the paper from his brother and glanced intently at the pictures, then back to Olivia. "I hardly ever say this, Luke, but…you're right. The resemblance is uncanny." He arched an eyebrow at Olivia. "Maybe you're Elvis's and Diana's love child."

Luke picked up on it right away; they were exceptionally quick with a joke, these twins. "And if she's the Princess of Wales and he's the King of Rock and Roll, that makes you—"

"The Princess of Welsh Rock," Olivia finished for them, and was gratified by the matching smiles of amusement on both twins' faces.

Fred grinned, motioning to her with the menu. "Well, Princess, what should we order for ye Royal dessert?"

Chapter Seven

Over the years, Olivia had kept in touch with both of the Connors twins on a regular basis, mostly through letters and e-mails. There had been promises made on both ends to visit, but life had too often gotten in the way. Still, somehow based on only that brief meeting in Boston, there had been enough of a connection to keep the friendship alive. When they'd learned of her acceptance to Oxford, the two boys had sent her flowers and a cardboard cutout of Elvis Presley by way of congratulations; in honor of their respective graduations from Northeastern and Emerson, she'd sent them quintessentially English care packages: Marmite, blood pudding, digestives, and jammie dodgers. Over the years, she'd come to treasure their back-and-forth jokes and correspondences, as brief and intermittent as they'd been.

So in a way, it wasn't at all surprising that seeing Fred Connors on her doorstep should dissolve her into a puddle of tears; but in another way, it was entirely remarkable, that she should feel so instantly safe and comforted in the presence of someone she'd only met in person once before.

Fred was quick to put her at ease, once she asked Janett to keep an eye on Miles so they could head to a nearby beachside café to catch up. "So," he said by way of breaking the awkwardness, "could be worse. You could have Charles's ears."

Olivia laughed, self-consciously touching her ears. "Truth was, I did when I was younger. I was so self-conscious about them that finally when I was ten, my parents let me go in to have them pinned back. That was actually the first time I ever saw Diana in person." She swallowed as the memory came back to her. "It was 199…1, I believe? The beginning of June. William had been hit accidentally by a golf club or something, and she rushed him in with a skull fracture. I barely saw her, only a glimpse of her, but I can remember it exactly in my mind."

She stopped, realizing that she'd drifted into territory of the morose. She tried her best to smile at Fred. Olivia was relieved that Fred's mention of Prince Charles's ear meant he knew that the Prince was her birth father. "Listen to what a bore I've become. You came all this way just to find me . . ." A sudden thought struck her. "What took you so long, anyway? I've been here for ages already."

Fred leaned back in his chair, arms folded across his chest. "I was deep undercover, which is why it took Eddie so long to get a hold of me. Eddie apparently read about me in your journals. He felt that since I was in the States I might be able to look over you. Eddie told me everything, who you are, Churchill, Daniel. Liv, I am so sorry."

Yes, Olivia could envisage that scenario in her mind. Fred had always been sharp-minded, but the years had filled him out, toughened him up a bit. She imagined he made quite the formidable force, with his boxer's lean muscularity and quick wit. "And Luke?"

"He's living here, actually, just ten minutes away, if you can believe it. Working as a broadcaster for the local evening news."

Olivia blinked in surprise. "Ten minutes away? Then how didn't Eddie manage to find him before now?"

Fred smiled, coupled with an affectionate eye roll. "Because he's going by his stage name." He allowed a beat for anticipation before revealing, "Luke Detroit."

Olivia pressed a hand to her mouth, half-horrified, half-amused. "No. Really?"

"Really," Fred confirmed with a nod. "Apparently it went over better with the test groups."

As Olivia giggled into her napkin, Fred fished out his wallet, withdrawing two pictures. "There's Luke with his Miss America wife and prerequisite 2.5 kids." His voice softened as he handed over the other photograph. "And there's my Jessica and our girls."

It was with a pang of reflexive jealousy that Olivia looked over the photographs. She'd always harbored something of a silly crush on the Connors twins—nothing that had ever been allowed to fully develop into anything serious, though the idea of them was something she held on a pedestal. Finding real love with Daniel had shown her just how silly those infatuations were, but some habits, it seemed, died hard.

The first photograph showed her that Luke, too, had changed over the years. He was not so muscular and tattooed as Fred, but sleeker, more TV-friendly, with hints of blonde highlights in his grown-out, wavy hair—courtesy of Daryl Drake, Boston's colorist of the rich and famous—though his eyes still sparkled with the familiar mischievous charm. His wife was platinum blonde and tan—Miss America, just as Fred had described her—and their two children, one boy and one girl, were dressed with impeccable fashion sense for children so young.

Fred's family could not have been more opposite. His wife was dark-haired and looked Latina, and his three daughters were presentable but not overly stylish. And judging by the looks they were giving to the camera, they came stocked with more than a little bit of attitude.

"Three girls?" Olivia asked, handing him back the photographs.

"And hellions, all of them," Fred returned proudly. "They'll sure have a thing or two to teach Luke's albino kids." He sobered a bit, shaking his head. "Actually, I give him a hard time, but things haven't been easy for Luke and his wife. They struggled for years with infertility. Their daughter, Paige, was actually adopted. And they were only able to have their son, Ethan, with help from . . . your father."

Olivia's eyes filled instinctively at the mention of her father Arthur, who had been murdered in an attempt to silence the truth about her bloodline. Fred's face softened, and he reached across the table for her hand. "Eddie filled me in on everything that happened including your true identity. Olivia, I'm so sorry to hear about your parents."

"Thank you," Olivia managed, swallowing back what remained of her tears. She thought about confiding to him about Daniel, but it seemed too soon for that; the pain was too fresh to talk about it with anyone, even Fred.

His brow still creased with concern, Fred continued to watch her. "These people are never going to stop coming after you, Princess. I wish you'd come back with me to Boston. I could get you set up in the witness protection program, make sure the best guys are on your case, keep an eye on you myself . . ."

"I can't." Olivia brushed at her eyes with the back of her hand. "I can't leave Miles."

A few minutes later, Fred insisted on walking her back to the house, promising in the meanwhile that he would get in touch with Luke and give the three of them a proper reunion. "But only if you promise to tease him mercilessly about his new name," Fred bargained.

Olivia grinned in return, crossing her heart with her fingers—a left-over reflex from all her time spent with a seven-year-old. "I swear it."

They reached the beach house just as a car pulled up in front and a man emerged: John Bradford Verner, all six-foot-four of him. As always, he was dressed impeccably, not a crease or wrinkle to be found on his expensive Italian suit, and not one single dark hair out of place.

Olivia stopped in her tracks, so abruptly that Fred bumped into her from behind. "Hey!" he protested, drawing the weight of Verner's searing blue gaze upon them.

For what seemed like an eternity, Verner stared at Olivia without seeming to recognize her. And then he blinked, his face blank, reflecting neither pleasure nor distaste at the sight of her. "Ms. Spencer? I thought you were meant to be with Miles."

As usual, Olivia found her composure melting in the face of this hard, intimidating man. "I am. I *was*. Janett's with him now; I just had to step out for a briefly . . ."

Verner's eyes narrowed in on Fred, standing in behind her; and though it had seemed impossible a moment before, his face seemed to grow even harder, his eyes cooler. "I see."

Stepping out from behind Olivia, Fred extended his hand, wearing his trademark broad smile. "How you doin'? I'm Fred Connors."

Dear, amiable Fred probably thought he could smooth things over with a little friendliness; but if anything, his effort only seemed to make things worse. Verner looked him over with thinly veiled annoyance, making no move to take his hand before returning his cool gaze to Olivia's. "Am I to understand that I've been ungenerous with the amount of leisure time I give you?"

Olivia squirmed under the weight of his gaze. She'd faced down far worse in the last few years of her life, and yet somehow he always managed to make her feel like a bumbling teenager, unable to find her wits or her tongue. "No, of course not—"

"Then from now on, I trust you'll actually work when I'm paying you to do so."

She swallowed. "Of course, Mr. Verner."

Verner held her gaze for a minute longer before abruptly turning on his heel and striding up toward the house. Waiting until he was inside, Olivia finally released the breath she'd been holding. "Pompous, insufferable man."

When she looked back to Fred, it was to find him watching her with a knowing smile. She narrowed her eyebrows. "What?"

"Oh, nothing." Fred motioned toward the house with his head. "Just remembering back in the day when I used to get my wife that riled up before she realized she was crazy for me."

Olivia scoffed. "Why do men always think when we can't stand to look at them that we're actually head-over-heels in love? Sometimes we actually just don't like you very much."

Seeing the deepening smile on Fred's face, she continued, "Besides which, he's engaged. To a Miss Samantha Emerson." Olivia couldn't quite keep the distaste out of her voice at the mention of the woman's name. *Snooty Samantha*, as she always referred to her in her mind—though Fred would no doubt misinterpret that as jealousy if she mentioned it out loud. "I'm not sure *how*, since the man has a lump of coal in place of a heart, but there you go. Moot point."

"Okay," Fred said as he backed up toward the street, hands held up in surrender. "Sounds like you've convinced yourself, so that's good enough for me."

But he sounded anything but persuaded, and his eyes sparkled with mischief. Despite herself, Olivia cracked a smile, shaking her head. "Pompous wanker."

"Love you, too, Princess," Fred called as he ducked into his car, sending off one last wave before driving out of sight.

"I don't understand how someone without military resources or training could just *disappear* so completely."

R.W. Curran bit back his own frustration. Truth be told, he didn't understand it either, though that didn't make it any less frustrating that Olivia Franklin had somehow managed to avoid him all this time. He'd heard that she bore a strong resemblance to her biological mother, but it seemed she had even more in common with Diana than just that. They were ghosts, the both of them, impossible to track down, and just as impossible to forget.

"She must be getting some kind of help that we don't know about," Curran explained in his most patient tone. "But sooner or later, she's bound to slip up. I will find her, Your Highness."

"I've been hearing that for months now, Curran. You'll forgive me if it's started to lose some of its credibility."

Curran whetted his lips. "It might be easier if..." He trailed off, waiting for his employer to take the bait.

A long pause. "If?" he prompted at last.

Bracing himself against the wall in his hotel room, Curran continued, "I know your original plan was for me to bring her back alive. But with someone so adept at running and disappearing... If you really want her silenced, sir, your best option might be for me to take the shot when I have the chance."

Another long pause, during which he could hear the sound of his employer's labored breathing. "Of course, I can't officially give such an order."

Curran smiled despite himself. He'd dealt with enough bureaucratic red tape to understand what that meant. "I understand."

"If this were ever traced back to me—"

"It won't be," Curran reassured him. "I give you my word…Prince Charles."

Chapter Eight

"And then . . .?" Miles prompted, giggling.

Olivia couldn't help but laugh along with him, his giggles proving to be contagious. "And then the dragon whipped out his scuba gear—"

Another fit of laughter from the boy. "No!" he squealed in protest.

"Busted out his mad ninja skills?" Olivia tried.

"No!"

"Danced onstage at the opera with a pink frilly tutu?"

Soon they were both laughing too hard to continue. Olivia knew she shouldn't be riling him up right before bedtime, but sometimes moments like these were too precious to pass up. He reminded her so much of some of the children she'd worked with in Zimbabwe. Most of those children had endured horrific experiences, much as she had herself, and for that matter, little Miles, too; but still, they reached for hope. Laughter. Joy. Those were the things that made life worth living that kept the nightmares at bay.

Some nights, it was enough for Olivia. Some nights, she still saw Daniel's face.

"All right, little monkey," Olivia said affectionately once the last fit of giggles finally subsided, "time for sleep."

Miles protested it for as long as he could, but soon he was yawning so much that even he could no longer deny the need for bed. As always, he asked Olivia to stay with him until he fell asleep. She wondered if he, too, saw images he'd rather not see behind his closed eyes: dark, churning water, and his mother's headless corpse floating nearby.

Suppressing a shudder, Olivia sang softly and stroked Miles's hair off his forehead until his eyes began to drift shut. Just when she thought it was safe to leave, his small fingers closed around her thumb, holding her in place. "You won't ever leave me, will you, Melissa?" he mumbled.

Olivia swallowed back the lump in her throat. She'd always been careful not to make promises to Miles that she couldn't keep—because the truth was, at the first hint of danger, she knew she would have to leave him and never look back. Anything to keep him safe. But how to explain that to a child, when she could hardly grasp the injustice of it herself?

"I'll always love you," she promised him instead, because she knew in her heart it was true.

The floorboard in the hallway creaked. Olivia froze, immediately shifting her body so she was in front of Miles—but instead she caught a glimpse of John Verner, moving quickly in the other direction.

She frowned, staring after him. Had he been watching them? Eddie had been the one to recommend that she come here, and had vouched for Verner himself, so in theory she knew he must be trustworthy; but she always felt on edge around him, like she was under constant scrutiny. He had made it very clear that he didn't like her, that he could hardly stand to be in the same room as her, and yet—

His eyes seemed to follow her everywhere she went. Those cold blue eyes, which with a little more softness might have been striking, even... beautiful.

Stupid, Olivia berated herself, shaking her head. He was an engaged man who had made it all too clear that he wanted nothing to do with her. More to the point, she wanted nothing to do with him—proud, arrogant, insufferable man, with his snooty, arrogant, insufferable fiancé.

Behind her, Miles gave a soft little sigh, finally lost into the land of dreams. Placing a soft kiss to his forehead, Olivia detangled herself from his grip and silently slipped from the room.

Chapter Nine

John Verner cranked up the incline on his treadmill, determined to push through his annoyance and clear his head. He'd been absolutely furious to come home and find Melissa canoodling with that tattooed low-life on his front porch. Anyone else he would have let go for abandoning his son to meet up with her boyfriend; but Miles absolutely adored her, and instances like tonight—watching her whisper and giggle with his son like they were best friends, joined at the hip—reminded him why he hadn't fired her on the spot. That, and because Eddie Armstrong had asked for his help, and for Julia's sake, John couldn't very well refuse him.

Julia. At the thought of his dead wife, John cranked up the speed on the treadmill another notch or two. For the first few years after the accident, he'd been unable to think of her without being reminded of the horrible image of her body laid out on the examination table for him to identify. For some reason, having Melissa around seemed to have opened the door for him to remember his wife, as she'd been before. The woman he loved.

In many ways, he reluctantly admitted to himself, Melissa and Julia were very much the same. Both were British, well educated, tall, and slender—though Julia had been blonde; John had always had a thing for blondes. Although, he again reluctantly admitted to himself, Melissa's short dark hair suited her, highlighting her fair skin and the dark chocolate-brown of her eyes. More importantly, Melissa was *warm*, just like Julia had been warm, and kind, just as Julia had been kind—though somehow he couldn't shake the feeling with Melissa that she was secretly judging him, finding that he measured up short. It was no secret to anyone that he hadn't been the world's best father since Julia's death; but he loved his son fiercely, whole-heartedly, and anyone who thought otherwise was wrong. Things had just been so much easier with Julia around. Life had been so much easier. Sometimes he found it almost unbearable without her by his side.

At least he had Samantha now, he reminded himself. Samantha was beautiful, intelligent and very Palm Beach. She always knew the right thing to say.

Finally, the workout cycle came to an end. Overcome by his still pent-up energy, John had just started to program in another run when something caught his attention. Lights, coming from the back yard, in the direction of what would be...

John's heart stopped. No. It couldn't be.

In two short strides, he had reached the window, peering out cautiously, his heart in his throat. Yes, there were lights coming from the yacht—the one that had sat untouched and unused since Julia's accident three years before.

"Get a hold of yourself, Verner," John muttered to himself. "This isn't *Wuthering Heights*."

No, this wasn't a ghost story, and that wasn't his dead wife's spirit coming back to haunt him. As he focused through the dark, he could make out the shape of someone climbing through the boat, and the single beam of a flashlight bobbing along.

Hands clenched into fists at his side, John pivoted, determined to put a stop to whoever dared disturb the memory of what he had worked so hard to put to rest.

Olivia had just slipped underneath her covers and pulled out her book when the realization struck her: Miles's shoes. He'd taken them off earlier that afternoon when they were building sandcastles, and as far as she could remember, they hadn't been in his hands when they came back up for dinner. Normally she wouldn't have worried about it, would have just gone down to fetch them in the morning, but with the high-climbing tide, they would probably be gone by then. And after Mr. Verner had caught her out with Fred that afternoon, she didn't want to give him yet another reason to give her that cold, vaguely disdainful look of disapproval.

With a sigh, she slipped back out of bed, grabbing a pair of flip-flops and a sweater to throw on over her silk camisole and shorts. With any luck, she'd find the shoes easily and be back inside before she even had a chance to catch a chill, but it didn't hurt to have a little added protection.

It took a little maneuvering in the dark, but she finally located the sandals, dangerously near the fast-approaching tide. She snatched them and pivoted back toward the house—when something caught her eye. The yacht, which Janett had informed her hadn't been used since Julia's untimely death. Olivia had always been vaguely curious about the boat but had never had a reason to venture any closer to it. But it was late, and nobody else was awake . . . and a little exploring had never hurt anybody.

Casting a quick glance toward the house to make certain nobody was watching her, Olivia made her way to the railing of the beached boat, hoisting herself aboard.

She made her way inside the pitch-black cabin, not sure what she was expecting to find, but curious all the same. Bumping into a desk, her hands fumbled across it until they found something that felt like a flashlight. She switched it on, swinging it across the room to see what secrets she might uncover.

There was nothing all that remarkable, save for the amount of dust that had gathered for want of use. Everything else in the cabin seemed fairly run-of-the-mill—no trap doors or secret mad ogres hidden below deck. The only thing of real interest was the corkboard behind the desk, brimming with pushpins and pictures. Olivia stepped in to examine them a little more closely. She realized with a start that she'd never seen a picture of Julia before—Mr. Verner must have had all of them removed from the house. She was a beautiful woman, with a clever, mischievous twinkle to her eye that reminded Olivia very much of Eddie. In all of the pictures, she was laughing, smiling, but never so much as when she was looking at John.

Olivia couldn't recall a time that she'd actually seen Mr. Verner smile, but in these photographs he was beaming, his face softened and unmarred with lines of grief. He had clearly loved her very much.

Feeling suddenly despicable for snooping around, Olivia had just turned to leave when suddenly she came face-to-face with the man himself—John Verner, who was not smiling now, but fuming.

Olivia felt her mouth run dry. "I'm so sorry. I didn't mean to . . ." But how to explain away what she'd been doing? She'd been in the wrong, and she knew it, only she'd been so curious. Mr. Verner never talked about Julia, never so much as mentioned her name. It was if the memory of her had disappeared along with her the day she died.

"You have no right to be in here," Verner seethed at her, his eyes two pinpoints of sharp, angry blue.

"I know, I'm sorry—"

"Do you have no respect for other people's privacy? Or should I start bursting into your room in the middle of the night and looking through your things?"

Olivia took a step back and up. John stepped in and closer so that the two of them were virtually chest-to-chest now. Despite the seriousness of the situation, Olivia felt her breath catch in her throat. John Verner had always seemed such a distant, cold imposing figure—but up close, he was far from cold. He was searing, blazing hot.

She swallowed, hard. "I was only—"

Verner's blazing eyes darted down from her eyes to her lips, lingering for just one second too long, and Olivia lost all ability to speak. *Get a hold of yourself,* she berated herself internally. *You can't stand this man, remember? He's odious.*

But somehow, treacherously, her heart was still racing. In a blind panic, she tried to break away, making for the door. Before she could reach it, Verner grabbed her by the wrist, dragging her back to him. "Don't walk away while I'm talking to you—"

Unbidden, the memory came to mind of being dragged from the jeep by the very men who had murdered Daniel right before her very eyes. With a bloodcurdling scream that Olivia hardly recognized as being her own, she wrenched free from Verner's grasp and ran off into the night.

Chapter Ten

A furious John Verner slammed the back door behind and raced up the stairs. The gall of that woman, breaking onto his private property and then acting as if he was assaulting her when he'd simply asked her a few questions. It had taken all of his willpower not to show that he'd registered her barely-there shorts, revealing her long beach-tanned legs in all of their glory, or her thin, virtually sheer camisole. Not an entirely prudent outfit for breaking and entering, he mused to himself bitterly.

One very long, very cold shower did little to calm John's fury at the situation. Slipping on his robe, he picked up his cell phone and found his brother-in-law in the contacts directory. He knew because of the time change from here to London that he'd be rousing Eddie out of bed, but he didn't care. He had dragged them into this mess by bringing this woman into their lives, and now he was going to hear about it.

A groggy-sounding Eddie picked up on the other end. "*What?*"

"Melissa Spencer," John growled into the phone. "The witness I've been helping you keep under low profile. Any chance you've actually sent me an international jewel thief, because tonight I found her rummaging through my things like she was casing the joint."

He had his brother-in-law's attention now. Eddie groaned into the phone, sounding much more lucid now. "First of all, no one says 'casing the joint' unless they're in a Bogart film, John. And second of all, I'm sure it was harmless."

"Harmless—?"

"Let me guess—you don't have a single picture of Julia hanging anywhere in the house. And no one's allowed to mention her, either. So you can't really blame Melissa for being curious about She-Who-Must-Not-Be-Named, can you?"

"That doesn't give her any right to go through my things." John continued to fume in silence, knowing Eddie was probably right but not wanting to give him the satisfaction of owning up to it. "Well, it goes both ways. I want to know who she is and why she's hiding out in my house."

"You know I can't tell you that, John."

"Not the specific details maybe," John persisted, "but it goes both ways. If she's going to dig through my past then I'm allowed to dig through hers."

A long awkward moment of silence followed. "Domestic abuse," Eddie returned finally. "You know I can't tell you any more than that, but trust me. It got pretty ugly."

John remembered the way Melissa had panicked when he'd grabbed her, and the sound of her awful, bloodcurdling scream. Sinking down on the edge of the bed, he buried his face in his hands. "Shit."

"So cut her a break, all right?" He could hear the exasperation in Eddie's voice loud and clear. "And let me get some sleep."

Olivia didn't know quite where she was going, only that she had to get away from the house, away from John Verner. Rationally she knew she shouldn't blame him for becoming so irate; she was the one who'd been in the wrong, after all. But another less logical part of her was furious. He'd been determined to hate her from the very beginning, and now he'd finally found a legitimate reason to fire her. It wasn't the money that concerned her; she still hadn't touched the $100,000 she deposited in the West Palm Beach bank. Also, she had quite a bit in savings from her parents. But Miles . . . what would she do if he took her away from Miles? Who would be left to love him then?

By the time she'd finished wandering, hours had passed, and with a start she realized she'd walked so far that she was no longer in Palm Beach, but Lantana. Lights on the street ahead alerted her to a 24-hour Walgreens up ahead. Pulling her sweater more tightly around her pajamas and hoping that no one would look too closely, she ducked inside.

She'd only meant to get out of the evening chill for a moment, take a minute to collect herself and gather her bearings.

And then she saw the magazine.

With her own picture peering back at her.

"Princess Diana's Secret Daughter" read the cover of the January 30th edition of the *Globe Magazine* tabloid, and underneath was her own face—or at least, a fairly good rendition of a digital artist's interpretation of what she would look like. With trembling hands, Olivia flipped through to find a full two-page story about some book that had been published about the secret daughter of Princess Diana and Prince Charles, *The Disappearance of Olivia.*

Her hands began to shake. How did anyone know about this? She and Eddie and Daniel had worked so hard to keep things covered up. Already there had been at least two men who would stop at nothing to make sure she died because of this very information. How many more would follow now that it was out there for the entire world to see?

Impulsively, Olivia grabbed the remaining magazines from the rack and shoved them inside her sweater, holding them in place as she made a break for the door.

Outside, she did not stop running until she reached the shore. It was irrational, she knew; other copies must exist, and stealing these six or seven magazines wouldn't accomplish anything in the long run. But somehow she knew she'd never be able to sleep, knowing her face—her true face—was there on the corner Walgreens for everyone to see.

With a pent-up scream of frustration, Olivia threw the magazines into the waves as hard as she could, watching as they were swallowed up by the dark, churning water.

Charles tried to keep his focus on the cricket match onscreen, but his attention kept being diverted by his sons William and Harry, who were pouring over something on William's mobile phone. It certainly wasn't the first time the two boys had been distracted by a humorous meme they found online; once at the Invictus Games, the three of them had been caught by the tabloids giggling over a particularly silly gifset William had shown them.

What was unlike them was to be so secretive. Perhaps it was something naughty, which is why they didn't want to share with their father. "All right, then," Charles spoke up finally, muting the television. "Let's see what it is."

William and Harry exchanged a glance. "Don't worry about it, Father," Harry spoke up finally, as William tried to subtly slip his phone back into his pocket. "It's rubbish anyway."

"I'll be the judge of that." Charles held out his hand, expectant. "Hand it over now. I mean it."

With a sigh, William reluctantly obliged. Charles kept his face stern, wanting to make them squirm a little bit before he finally joined in on the laughter. But what he saw on the mobile phone screen made his mouth run dry.

It was an article by one of those trashy magazines, all about Olivia Franklin. Charles gaped at it in horror for a moment, until at last the seething rage took over. Most people wouldn't take something like *The Globe* seriously, but if this wasn't taken care of, soon other news outlets would begin to pick up the story, and there would be no end to it. Then everything he'd built for his sons—his true children—and their future children, would be lost.

"She is our sister." It was William speaking up this time. "We just want to know that she's all right."

"You'd do better to worry about your own children," Charles snapped at him, fishing for his own phone. He'd pull a few strings with some of his contacts in the media, line a few pockets so the story didn't get picked up elsewhere. "What do you think will happen once Olivia decides she wants your money—their money?"

Harry shook his head. "She isn't like that. If you bothered to get to know her—"

"I don't need to get to know her!" Charles slammed William's phone down onto the coffee table, shattering it to pieces. "She is NOT my daughter."

The door opened and Kate poked her head in, looking from William to Charles and then back again. "Is everything all right? I heard shouting down the hall."

Too late, Charles realized how loudly he'd raised his voice. Doubtless the entire house had heard him now—all the servants.

Ignoring the pointed glance between his two sons, Charles stormed out of the room, shouldering past Kate in his haste to get away.

Olivia Franklin was trying to drive him mad. But he wouldn't let her; over his dead body—or better yet, hers.

Chapter Eleven

Back in the safety of her room—having thankfully avoided any further encounters with John Verner—Olivia quickly found *The Disappearance of Olivia* online at Amazon.com. The book had received great reviews and seemed to be flying off the shelves, but it was with hands trembling with dread and not anticipation that Olivia downloaded the e-book onto her iPad.

She read early into the morning, far past the time when her eyes had begun to burn with the strain of still being awake. The account was so vivid—and so incredible. It was exactly her life. Every word seemed to come from Olivia's journals. How was it possible that someone would know all of the intimate details of what had happened to her, of everything she had gained and everything she had lost?

And now a book was being promoted in a tabloid magazine. What would be next—newspapers? Television? She already had at least one person hot on her trail, trying to kill her. But how many more would it be once word had gotten out?

Overwhelmed, exhausted, and frightened, Olivia finally lowered her head to her pillow, allowing the sobs she had suppressed for so long to finally come to the surface.

She would never be safe, she was beginning to realize. Not as Melissa Spencer, not as Olivia Franklin.

Wherever she went, they would always find her.

John hesitated outside of Melissa's bedroom. He'd heard her slipping in a few hours before and had thought about going to her then, but realized it might be best to give her some more time to cool off.

No, that wasn't true at all he admitted, shaking his head ruefully. He was afraid to apologize to her. He, John Bradford Verner, self-made billionaire and renowned boardroom shark, was afraid to apologize to a governess. An admittedly beautiful, stubborn, strong-willed governess, but a governess nonetheless. This was getting ridiculous; he'd allowed her to take far too much hold over his life already.

Taking in a deep breath, John raised his hand to knock—when he heard muffled noises coming from within. Sobs, from the sound of it. Shit. He hadn't meant to frighten her that badly. It bothered him more than he could put words to that she would think he might hurt her.

Once more he hesitated, his hand hovering just above the door. Foregoing the knock, he cleared his throat. "Melissa?"

Inside the room, the sobs immediately ceased, replaced by an anticipatory silence.

"I . . ." John searched for the right words. He had never been much good at this sort of thing. Julia had always teased that trying to get him to apologize was like pulling teeth—out of a bear. "I'm . . . sorry."

Not the most eloquent speech of all time, but he meant it. He hoped Melissa knew that.

For a second, he waited half-hoping there might be some kind of response.

Silence was his only answer.

Sighing, John turned and retreated down the hallway.

Inside the room, Olivia listened with her ear pressed to the door, listening to the sound of his departing footsteps. Sighing, she sank down to the ground, pulling her sweater more tightly around herself for warmth.

Chapter Twelve

It was a mostly sleepless morning. Olivia tossed and turned, catching bits and snatches here and there, though almost all of her brief dreams twisted into nightmares, sending her into gasping wakefulness once more.

Finally at five o'clock she gave in and picked up her phone, dialing Eddie's carefully memorized number. For once, she was grateful for the time change that meant he would be awake and alert, and that she wouldn't have to wait any longer to speak to someone about the things she'd read.

Eddie answered on the second ring, sighing into the phone. "I thought you might be calling me."

Olivia frowned into the phone. Eddie almost constantly amazed her with his impeccable sixth sense, but this was stretching it a bit, even for him. "So you know about the book?"

It was Eddie's turn to sound confused. "What book?" Olivia quickly filled him in. As she finished, Eddie cleared his throat. "Ah, *that* book. I, um, actually did know about that one."

"And you didn't see fit to tell me about it?" Sometimes Olivia wanted to strangle the man, she really did.

"It was a fail-safe, Olivia. I had to make certain if anything happened to you or to me, the information would get out there. So, I contacted an old family friend. I shared with her your journals that I found in

Zimbabwe. I never imagined Nancy would actually *publish* it without my permission, mind you."

"Eddie!"

"This doesn't change anything, Olivia." Eddie did his best to soothe her with his voice, like he was talking to a rambunctious three-year-old throwing a temper tantrum. "Sure, the story's been leaked, but most people are still treating it like it's just that—a story, and that's the way we're going to keep it. You're still safe. Nobody knows where you are, and we're going to keep it that way, too. Okay?"

Olivia took in a deep breath, sighing into the phone. "Okay."

"I'm not going to let anything happen to you, kiddo. Trust me."

As soon as he'd hung up with Olivia, Eddie fell back in his chair. Tears filled his eyes. Eddie took Olivia's private journals from Africa and put them in what he thought was a safe place. Eddie never thought his assistant, Nancy, would read the journals let alone use them to create a self-published novel. What a nightmare.

Eddie dialed Fred Connors, impatiently waiting as it rang. Assuring Olivia that she was safe and sound had been the right thing to do; it would only worry her to know just how many problems that damn book had caused, or that the reason he'd sent Fred Connors down to Florida was because R.W. Curran was hot on Olivia's trail.

Fred answered after the fourth ring, groggy and irritated. "Ever heard of something called a sunrise? I generally prefer not to be awoken before that happens."

"Rise and shine, sweetheart. It's Eddie Armstrong."

That seemed to get Fred's attention. He cleared his throat, suddenly sounding much more alert. "What's going on? Is it Olivia?"

"Relax, Boston. She's fine for now. Just wanted to give you the heads up that Olivia knows about the book. But she doesn't know how close Curran is on her trail, and we're going to keep it that way."

Fred grunted. "You're right. Because I'm going to kill that son of a bitch before he has the chance to get within two miles of her."

Eddie set his mouth grimly. "Might be too late for that already. My Intel says that Curran's tracked Olivia as far as Florida. I'm heading out as soon as I can, but until I get there, I need to know you can keep her safe."

Fred swore under his breath. "Yeah, of course." A brief pause, as he seemed to mull over something in his mind. "Hey, you don't happen to have a picture of the guy, do you?"

Eddie furrowed his brow. "Might be able to scrape something up. Why?"

Fred waited outside the spacious condo, glancing surreptitiously through his sunglass shades to see one of the neighbors peering at him through the blinds. He raised his hand to wave, but the neighbor quickly ducked out of sight. "Lock up all your valuables," Fred muttered under his breath, reaching up to knock on the door again.

A moment later, it swung open, revealing a startled-looking Luke. "Freddy? What the hell are you doing here?"

"Nice to see you, too, brother." Fred motioned with his head toward the street. "Can you let me in? Neighborhood Watch has already marked me as a suspicious person."

"Maybe if you covered up a few of those tattoos . . ." But Luke obligingly stepped aside, letting him into the house. "So what brings you down to my fair state? I thought natural sunlight made you burst into flames."

"Ha-ha." Fred made his way into the kitchen, doing a brief check to make sure they were alone. "Sabrina out with the kids?"

"They had toddler gymnastics." At the look Fred gave him, Luke's own gaze soured. "Don't start."

Fred bit back a laugh, holding up his hands in surrender. "I didn't say anything." His mood sobered as he remembered the reason he'd come. "So, look. It's about Olivia."

Luke's face immediately flooded with concern. "Princess? Is she okay?"

Fred took in a deep breath. "Well, actually, no. She's . . . kind of a real princess . . ."

He described the whole ordeal to Luke. How Olivia had led what she believed to be a normal life, until someone attempted to kill her, setting off a chain of events that would change her life forever.

The man she believed to be her father, Arthur Franklin, had finally been forced to reveal the truth. As one of the leading fertility experts in the U.K., a very young woman had visited Arthur several years before. The woman called herself Mary Wagner. Ms. Wagner explained to Arthur that she needed to prove her fertility before her upcoming engagement would be announced. Ms. Wagner had to provide Dr. Franklin with a sample of her future fiancé's semen, as well as her own eggs. Only her bodyguard, a man by the name of Philip Churchill, accompanied the woman.

At the time, Arthur's own wife had been struggling with her inability to conceive. When Mary Wagner's sample proved viable, Arthur was meant to destroy the viable embryo—but instead, he'd inseminated his wife Elizabeth, who believed it to be a donation, a wonderful gift. It wasn't until Prince Charles's Royal engagement announcement that Arthur realized who Mary Wagner truly was: Diana Spencer, soon to be Princess Diana of Wales. But by then, Elizabeth was pregnant, and it was too late to reverse what had taken place.

It seemed they'd stayed safely under the radar until several years later when Olivia encountered Philip Churchill at a party. The man, who had once posed as "Mary Wagner's" bodyguard, was now head of the Royal Guard—and realizing what Arthur Franklin had done, took it as his own personal mission to bury this evidence of Charles's and Diana's true heir before anyone else could discover her.

In the process, countless people had been murdered, including Arthur and Elizabeth Franklin, and though Churchill himself had eventually been killed, Olivia had been forced to go on the run with her love, Daniel, once they discovered that Churchill's orders must have come from far higher up in the government—even from one of the Royals themselves.

"In short," Fred concluded, "she's been to hell and back. But we're going to make sure nothing bad ever happens to her again."

There was no need to ask the question; he knew Luke would be on his side. No matter how different the two of them might be, one thing they would always have in common was how much they loved Olivia. "What can I do?" Luke asked, tanned face uncharacteristically solemn and filled with shock.

Fred grinned, sliding a folder across the table to his twin. "I was hoping you'd ask."

"That's one lucky little dog," Luke, concluded the slice-of-life segment, beaming into the camera. He shuffled some papers on his desk, going into serious-reporter-mode. "In other news, Florida authorities are on high alert due to the presence of an international terrorist, R.W. Curran."

At his cue, the photograph of Curran was broadcast across the screen—and into millions of homes. Watching from the sidelines, Fred grinned to himself. Let that bastard try to sneak up on them now— they'd just ensured that he would be one of the most wanted—and most recognizable—men in the state of Florida.

"Curran is believed to have direct connections to foreign militants, including Al-Qaeda-"

which wasn't true, of course, but nothing like the mention of Al-Qaeda to put the public into a high-alert frenzy.

"—And is considered a highly dangerous individual. If you see this man, or have any information about him, please contact your local authorities immediately."

As the show cut to commercial, Luke glanced over at his twin, exchanging a brief nod. Fred folded his arms over his chest. Curran might be the cat chasing the mouse—but they were big dogs, and now the whole neighborhood would be barking if Curran had the audacity to come slinking in.

Chapter Thirteen

Curran pulled his rental car into the nearest gas station, filling up the tank as he slipped inside to use the water closet. It was only a matter of time now. He was a half hour outside of Palm Beach, and from there it would be short work to find Olivia Franklin. He'd assured Prince Charles that he would be able to find her, and of course he had; he was the best, after all. But it had been a pleasant surprise that she'd led him here. Now he'd be able to work on his tan after putting a bullet through her pretty little head.

Finishing up in the toilet, Curran walked around the store, stretching his legs a bit and perusing through the snacks. He grabbed a pack of crisps and headed up to the register, waiting as a tubby truck driver finished up his purchase of a hot dog and three packs of Twinkies. *Americans.*

Finally it was his turn. Curran dropped the crisps onto the counter, pulling out a couple dollar bills and handing them over. As the cashier rang up the purchase, Curran's eyes fell upon the newspapers stacked up on the counter—and he froze at the sight of his own gaze starting back at him.

Doing his best to look nonchalant, Curran picked up the top newspaper and folded it under his arm, picture carefully out of sight, and grabbed a "Palm Beach" baseball cap. "Both of these, as well." He fished a twenty from his wallet, dropping it down on the counter. "Keep the change."

Back in his car, Curran drove a few blocks before parking on the side of a suburban street and unfolding the paper. As the major incriminating words popped out at him—*wanted, fugitive, terrorist*—he took in a deep breath through his nose.

"Shit."

Things had just gotten a hell of a lot more complicated.

Chapter Fourteen

"It needs another tower, right there!" Olivia examined the sandcastle she and Miles were constructing, feigning solemnity as she studied the structure. "Right there?" She pointed to the same spot he'd indicated only moments before, then pointed to a completely random spot sticking off the side. "Are you sure it shouldn't be right here?"

Miles rolled his eyes at her attempt at humor, though he was fighting a smile. "You're so weird, Melissa."

She laughed despite herself. "All right, I suppose we can manage another tower on top."

Miles went to work packing wet sand into a bucket as Olivia smoothed out the foundation. She snuck a few glances in his direction, touched as always by his seriousness and concentration on the task. "Do you think you'd like to do this when you're older? Be an architect?"

He furrowed his brow at her. "What's an architect?"

"Someone who designs buildings and then builds them."

Miles thought about it a brief second before shrugging his shoulders. "I dunno." All right, maybe a bit young to be mapping out his future. Olivia re-focused on the task at hand, waiting at the ready as Miles prepared to overturn the new tower. "All right, on the count of three. One, two—"

Miles whipped back the bucket, accidentally smacking Olivia in the eye. She reeled back, blinking back instinctive tears that welled in protest against the grain of sand now lodged firmly underneath her eyelid.

"Sorry, Melissa!" a frantic Miles kept repeating over and over again on a loop as she rose unsteadily to her feet.

Olivia did her best to smile at him. "It's fine, Miles. Really. I'll just go wash it out. Keep building for me, all right? I'll be right back . . ."

She managed to stumble her way into the house, still clutching at her eye. Making a beeline for the guest bathroom near the front door, she pushed her way inside, coming face-to-face with a very naked, very wet John Verner, fresh out of the shower.

"Oh my gosh." Olivia pivoted around, but not before she'd seen quite a bit more of her employer than she'd ever anticipated. So he did actually have a body underneath that suit. Funny, it was much more leanly muscular than she'd imagined. Not that she'd been imagining things . . .

"I am so sorry," she said to the wall. "There was sand in my eye, and I didn't think anyone else was home—"

She heard a faint rustling noise behind her, followed by John's deep voice, ever so slightly strained. "The exhaust fan wasn't working in mine upstairs. I should have locked the door . . ."

Olivia cursed herself inwardly. This was going to make things infinitely more awkward between the two of them. They'd barely spoken since the incident on the boat and his subsequent apology, aside from the usual *hello*, *how-are-you*, and *fine-thank-yous*. This was not anything too different from their normal routine, as they had never been particularly close, but now there was an added tension under the distance, a recognition that something had changed between them that night, though Olivia scarcely knew how to define it. And now . . .

Suddenly, a pair of warm, still-damp hands grasped her shoulders from behind, turning Olivia around. Verner had wrapped a towel around his lower half and reached out now to cup her chin. "Which eye?"

It took Olivia a full thirty seconds to process what was happening—fairly remarkable, considering how close and unclothed he was. "Oh, don't trouble yourself. I can just—"

"Which eye?" Verner repeated, and he was standing so close to her that she could feel the reverberations of it from his chest.

Olivia swallowed. "The left."

He stepped in even closer, peering. Olivia tried her best to remain still, to appear calm, but her heart was racing. He *was* a handsome man, she had to begrudgingly admit, and she was only human for noticing that.

"I don't see anything."

Olivia blinked in surprise, meeting Verner's gaze full on and startled, once more, by just how close he was. "The eye looks a little red and irritated, but I don't see any sand."

"I must have cried it out already." Olivia knew she should try to pull away but found, somehow, she couldn't. Mouth suddenly feeling like the Sahara desert, she wetted her lips, intending to say something clever, but losing all train of thought when she saw John's eyes follow the movement of her tongue.

His lips twitched, ever so slightly, and she stared. Was he actually smiling? "I guess I'll have to buy a bigger house to avoid this kind of awkward situation next time."

Olivia couldn't help but laugh at the absurdity of finding *anything* bigger than this gargantuan beast of a mansion. "Or learn how to deadbolt the loo."

"Ahem."

In surprise, both looked up to see a tall, pale, raven-haired woman standing in the doorway, arms folded over her chest.

Samantha Emerson—John Verner's fiancé.

At almost the same time, Olivia and Verner pulled apart from one another, as if shocked by matching bursts of electricity.

Verner blinked in surprise at the woman. "Samantha. What are you doing here?"

Samantha arched one perfectly sculpted eyebrow. "Don't you think *I* should be asking the questions here, John?"

"This isn't what it looks like." Olivia immediately wished away the words; the people who said that in the movies were always guilty, weren't they? "I had sand in my eye and—"

Samantha cut her off with a wave of her hand. "I think I caught the tail end of it. Door unlocked, you stumbled in, and a delightful little moment of domestic drama ensued." She was smiling as she said it, but she did not sound amused. Not even in the slightest.

Abruptly, she turned to Verner, ignoring Olivia as if she wasn't even there. "I tried calling you at the office, but they said you were playing hooky. So I thought I'd bring the fun to you." She brandished a bottle of wine. "What do you say we order in some caviar and go for a dip?"

Verner smiled in return, though his eyes didn't match it. "Well, actually, I left work early because I was planning on spending the day with Miles."

Olivia couldn't help but glance at him in surprise. John Verner was not the type of man to take off a day of work, and especially not to spend time with his son. She knew he cared about the boy, in his own distant way, but he'd always been more of a hands-off father. At least, from what she'd seen for herself, though pictures in various albums suggested things had been different, when Julia was still alive. Was it possible that John was changing...?

Samantha furrowed her brow, seeming—as always—to be taken aback by Miles's existence. "Oh, of course. Miles." She brightened her tone, though Olivia could still hear the strain in it. "Well, why don't the three of us make a day of it—you, me, and the little one?" She waved her manicured hand in Olivia's direction. "I'm sure Melissa would love to have the afternoon off, wouldn't you Melissa?"

Olivia glanced over to find Verner's gaze upon her, probing. "It's up to you, of course. I don't mind staying on if you need me." "Don't be silly!" Samantha cooed before Verner could speak up. "There's two of us and only one of him. I'm sure we'll manage." She leaned in closer to Olivia, lowering her voice to a conspiratorial whisper. "Besides which, Melissa dear, you're looking a bit rough around the edges. You could use a mani-pedi, dear. And a haircut wouldn't hurt."

Olivia felt a hot flush of anger and embarrassment rise into her cheeks. If she'd met Samantha as Dr. Olivia Franklin, she would have wiped the floor with the other woman. But as Melissa Spencer, governess, there was little she could say to her employer's fiancé. So, she bit her tongue. "How *kind* of you, Miss Emerson."

And, avoiding the impulse to glance back at John Verner one last time, she slipped out of the bathroom and headed up to her room to change.

Samantha quickly began to regret her promise of spending all afternoon with John's son. She had thought that surely at some point Miles would run out of energy and that she and John would get some much-needed alone time together; but if anything, she was the one starting to lag as the little boy ran circles around the adults.

Wrapping her arm through John's and leaning in closer, Samantha murmured, "Isn't it about time for him to take a nap?"

John only gave a short, vaguely irritated laugh. "He's seven."

As if that was supposed to mean something to her? Samantha released her hold on him, stepping away and holding her hands up in the air. "Sorry. I just thought it might be nice for the two of us to have some time alone together. You've been working so much lately."

And rushing home afterward every chance you get, she added to herself silently. John might think he was being subtle; in fact, it was entirely possible he truly had no idea that he was developing feelings for the new governess, but it hadn't been difficult for Samantha to piece together that a large part of John's new doing-things-as-a-family attitude had popped up right about the time the attractive brunette moved into their home.

Melissa Spencer. There was something about the woman that Samantha didn't trust, and it had nothing to do with her long, lithe legs—well, at least not entirely. What was such an educated, attractive, cultured woman doing working as a governess? She'd tried to question John on the subject, but he had been evasive—another clue that any woman worth her salt would know meant danger. The less a man wanted to talk about a woman, the more he was thinking about her, she'd learned from considerable experience.

John sighed, reaching out a conciliatory hand to her. "I'd like that, too." Taking her proffered palm, he kissed it. "But today is about Miles. I took the day off work specifically to spend more time with him."

Despite herself, Samantha felt her hackles rising. "So I'm getting in the way, is that it?" Funny, he hadn't seemed to mind having Melissa along as a third wheel.

"Of course not," John protested, but it sounded hollow, at best.

Samantha was still fuming, but knew she'd need to change tactics. Men in general—but John Verner in particular—did not react well to nagging, shrewish women. Especially with the idea of Melissa Spencer floating in his head. Well, Samantha wasn't going to go down without a fight.

"Forgive me, darling. I'm being horrible." She slid up to him, pressing the full length of her body against his as she leaned up on her tiptoes to kiss him. "Why don't I let you and Miles have the rest of the afternoon to yourselves—just the two boys? Then tonight after he goes to sleep, I can come by and give you one of my special massages."

She ran her hands over the length of his back, dipping a bit lower as she smiled at him suggestively. John smiled back at her. "Why are you so good to me?"

Samantha gave him one quick peck on the lips. "Don't you forget it." She said it lightly, like it was a joke, but in truth, it was a promise. She had worked too hard to win John Verner as her prize, and she would be damned some British floozy slipped in and stole him away.

Chapter Fifteen

For the third time in a week, Olivia finished reading *The Disappearance of Olivia*. At first the book had been nothing but a painful reminder to her of everything she'd gone through; but now, in many ways, it had proved to be a balm, reminding her of all the things she'd gained as well as what she'd lost. Getting to know her brothers and Kate was something she wouldn't trade for the world. Even though it was too dangerous to be in contact with them right now, both for them and for her, she continued to hold out hope that someday this would no longer be the case.

Just as importantly, it had reminded her of all the wonderful times she'd been able to spend with Daniel. She'd loved him for so long and had him for such a short amount of time, but how many people got to experience a love like that? That knowledge was a bittersweet thing. Even knowing how ultimately short her time with Daniel would prove to be, she was confident she wouldn't have given it up. But now she could not help but wonder if that kind of love only came along once in a lifetime. Lightning didn't strike twice, after all.

That melancholy train of thought was interrupted by a low, rumbling growl in her stomach. Olivia couldn't help but laugh out loud at the unexpectedness of it, glancing at the clock. It was three o'clock in the morning! Her stomach must be a bit confused. Best to just go to sleep and try to realign herself in the morning.

But despite her best attempts to fall asleep, Olivia's stomach persisted on insisting how much it wanted food. Finally, unable to resist any longer, she threw off the covers. "Fine," she grumbled to herself, "but don't blame me when you're exhausted in the morning . . ."

The house was silent, dark, as it should be at such an ungodly hour of the morning. Olivia slipped into the kitchen, trying not to make too much noise as she rifled through the fridge and cabinets. She was normally a fairly healthy eater, but for some reason it was difficult to remind her stomach of that at three in the morning. All she was craving were baked goods, crisps, pizza, and popcorn—the kinds of things she would definitely be regretting in the morning.

Unfortunately—or perhaps fortunately, depending on the perspective—John Verner was even more meticulous about healthy eating than she was. There was not a single trans-fat to be found in any of the cupboards, nor any gratuitous sugar. Sighing, Olivia was debating between a box of raisins or some gluten-free crackers when the kitchen light switched on.

Like a deer in the headlights, Olivia froze, turning to see an equally startled John Verner in a thin tee and a pair of boxer shorts.

For a moment, the two simply stared at one another. Then a guilty Olivia admitted, "I was hungry." John smiled in response—a slow, curling, dimpled grin that sent something fluttering in the pit of Olivia's stomach. "Me, too." He ventured a bit further into the room, motioning toward her. "Nice haircut."

One of Olivia's hands fluttered to her hair—cut and styled during the unexpected afternoon off. She hadn't expected anyone to notice, least of all John Verner. She hadn't realized he looked that closely. "Just a trim, nothing too fancy."

He met her gaze, held it, making a move as if to reach out and touch it but seeming to think better of it. "It looks nice."

Olivia felt her knees weaken in response. *Get a hold of yourself, Olivia,* she chastised herself sharply. *You're acting like a besotted teenager.*

Taking in a deep breath, she attempted to quell her nervousness by pretending there was nothing more natural in the world than a late-night rendezvous with her boss. "Unfortunately, the only thing to eat in this house is cardboard."

John laughed, shaking his head. "Leftover rules from Julia's reign. She studied nutrition in college and had very strong opinions about not poisoning our son's body, and I guess some things stuck." He crooked a finger at Olivia, motioning her toward him. "If I show you a secret, promise not to tell?"

Grinning back, Olivia crossed her heart with her fingers and twisted an imaginary key at her lips.

John put his shoulder to the refrigerator; wedging it aside just enough that he could reach in back and pull out a shoebox. Inside were an assortment of goodies—microwave popcorn, bags of crisps, candy bars, a sleeve of Oreos.

"Junk food!" Olivia cried, delighted.

Instantly, they were sitting at the kitchen table opposite one another, dunking Oreos into their respective glasses of milk. Olivia laughed as John recounted a story from his university days of driving around with his friends at 2:00 in the morning, trying to find a pizza place that was still open.

"…So we finally convince him to open up, only to realize that he's totally out of mozzarella," John concluded, shaking his head ruefully. "So we ended up just buying a frozen one and cooking it in the oven ourselves."

Olivia wiped at her eyes. "Sounds like a very American experience. Most of the shops in town closed around eight or nine, though there was a curry place that was open until 10—for all of the night owls roaming the streets."

"Where did you go to school?"

Olivia froze at the question, debating whether or not she should answer. Lots of people studied at university; surely that wouldn't be something that could give away her true identity? "Um . . . Oxford, actually."

"Oxford?" John's eyebrows raised; he looked impressed. "And now you're putting that schooling to good use by being my governess?"

She shrugged. "It isn't what I dreamt of, maybe, but . . . I love Miles. My time here with him has been some of the best of my life."

Every word was true, Olivia realized as she said it out loud. She had loved her time at school, loved working in the hospital in Oxford, loved being with the orphans in Zimbabwe, and Daniel . . . but right from the start, Miles had touched a special place in her heart that she'd thought had been broken past mending. There wasn't anything she wouldn't do for that boy.

When she looked back up at John again, she saw that his face had softened. How was it possible that she had once found him so frightening and cold and intimidating? "Miles loves having you here, too. I can't tell you what a godsend you've been."

He paused, seeming to be struggling to find the right words. "I know I haven't been the easiest on you . . . but I guess a part of me kept expecting Julia would come back, and then when she didn't, I blamed it on you. But you've changed things here, Melissa. You've made them so much better."

Listening to him, Olivia felt like her heart might burst. And then it struck her all at once. She was falling in love with this man. Even a week ago, she would have laughed at the idea, said it was impossible . . . but now she could see she'd been fighting it all along, from the very beginning.

John's eyes were earnest as they met hers. "Melissa, I—"

Someone cleared her throat from the doorway. Olivia looked up to see Samantha, wearing nothing but one of John's button-up shirts, smiling one of her saccharine smiles—though her eyes were shrewd and hard. "Am I interrupting something?"

A guilty Olivia turned her body away from John's. "We were just hungry."

"Mmm. Me, too." Samantha padded into the kitchen, stopping behind John's chair and placing a possessive hand on his shoulder as she used the other to dunk an Oreo into his glass of milk. "Yummy."

The message couldn't be more loud and clear. Samantha and John were in love—engaged, for goodness sake! —And Olivia was an idiot. Forcing out some excuse about being tired, she rose to her feet and hurried out of the room, not bothering to look back.

Chapter Sixteen

Settling herself back on her sun bed at the Mar-a-Largo Club, Samantha waved over the waiter. "A margarita—and don't be stingy with the tequila," she snapped at him before shooing him off again.

She was still fuming about what had happened the night before— or rather, early that morning. The nerve of John, to allow her to massage and pamper and oil him—and then to sneak off the second she fell asleep to cavort with the governess in the kitchen. If he'd already been her husband, she would have given him a good slap for that one. As it was, she would just have to keep playing nice until after the wedding, at which point Melissa would suddenly find herself in search of new employment.

That was, if they made it that far. Samantha had known for some time now that John had a crush on Melissa, even if he didn't realize it himself; but from what she'd seen of last night, that feeling had grown into something much deeper, and much more dangerous. What would he have said to her if she hadn't walked in and interrupted? The thought made Samantha shudder. Three months away from the wedding, and it looked like she was going to have to fight tooth, claw, and nail to make sure it even happened.

It was enough to warrant at least two poolside margaritas, she decided bitterly.

Her sun was blocked as someone came to stand over her. Speak of the devil. Samantha opened her eyes, expecting to see the waiter returned with her drink—but instead it was another man, older but athletically built and trim, but definitely not dressed for a day at the pool in his khakis, loafers, and polo. He wore a pair of dark-tinted sunglasses and a baseball cap that looked brand-new and out of place, as though he'd purchased it on impulse at a gift shop.

Seeing he'd caught her attention, he smiled. "Mind if I join you?" He had a British accent—educated, clipped, and precise.

Samantha gave him another quick, appraising look before allowing a slow, seductive smile. What John didn't know wouldn't hurt him, after all. "Sure. I'm always in search of good company."

The man took the sun bed next to hers, though he pulled the back up so that he wasn't reclining at all, and angled the overhead umbrella so that he wouldn't catch any extra sun. "You're Samantha Emerson, aren't you? John Verner's fiancé?"

Samantha's smile wavered. Well, there went her fun for the afternoon. "Sounds like someone's been doing his homework. And who, pray tell, are you?"

Was it only her imagination, or did the man hesitate for a moment? "James. James Quinn. I'm a private investigator, looking for a woman named Olivia Franklin. Ring any bells?"

How boring. Not only was he here on business, but also it was business about something that had absolutely nothing to do with her. Samantha sighed, rolling over onto her stomach. "Not particularly. Is she a member of the club, or something?"

"Maybe this will jog your memory." Quinn reached into his pocket, producing a photograph.

Out of courtesy, Samantha glanced at the photograph and was about to tell the investigator she had no idea who the woman was and hint very strongly that she'd like some quiet time—when suddenly, she did a double take. It was Melissa. The hair was blonde, the eyes color lighter, but there was no mistaking her unique, defined bone structure, the way she held her head.

Samantha sat up, taking the photograph from Quinn. "This is John's son's governess. But she's going by a different name now—Melissa Spencer."

Quinn made a clucking noise, shaking his head. "I imagine she would, after what she did."

Samantha searched his gaze hungrily. "Why? What did she do?"

"You name it." Quinn began ticking things off on his fingers. "Embezzlement, money laundering . . .even second-degree murder. And she's been running for a very long time. Any help you could give us would be very much appreciated."

Samantha could not help the crocodile grin that spread across her face. "Oh, I think I can manage. It is my civic duty, after all . . ."

Chapter Seventeen

"Race you back to the house!"

Miles abruptly released Olivia's hand and raced up the sidewalk toward the front door. She laughed, shaking her head after him, her hands on her hips. "No fair! Cheater!"

A grinning Miles touched the door triumphantly. "Slow poke!" he called back at her, sticking out his tongue.

Just as Olivia reached the front drive, a car pulled up toward the garage. John—Mr. Verner. Her stomach did a flip of protest as she braced herself to see him. Ever since Samantha's intervention the other evening, things had gone mostly back to normal between them, in that she hardly ever saw him and they were never alone together. Samantha had seen to that, inviting herself to swallow up any free moment John had. Olivia didn't know if it was just wishful thinking, but it seemed to her that John was growing increasingly irritated by Samantha's unannounced arrivals—not the kind of reaction one would expect from a man who was supposedly besotted . . .

Stop it. Olivia halted that train of thought before it could start. No amount of wishful thinking could change the facts: that John and Samantha were engaged, and that he was a full-grown man who could have changed that situation at any point if he was unhappy with it, and he hadn't. So it was time to stop acting like some sort of silly, twitter-pated schoolgirl.

She forced a bright smile as John emerged from the car, holding up a hand to shield the sun from her eyes. "You're home early."

The returning smile was even more blinding than the sun, causing Olivia's heart to go into overdrive. *Stop it*, she warned herself again. "The afternoon was too nice to be cooped up in an office. So I thought I'd come home and play some Frisbee." He glanced back at Miles, still waiting at the door. "How does that sound!"

"Yeah!" Miles raced inside. "I'll go get it!"

Laughing, John turned back to Olivia. "I just need to go change and then I'll meet you both out back."

Olivia felt a small surge of warmth, pleased to be included. "All right. But I should caution you that I'm an excellent Frisbee player, so you should probably prepare yourself to—how do you Americans say it? 'Have your ass handed to you on a plate'?"

John threw back his head and laughed. "Oh, so that's how it's going to be, is it?"

"I'm just warning you, that's all. Fair play, and all that."

John folded his arms over the chest, game to the challenge. "Well, I'll have you know that I used to blow off classes in college to play with my friends, so consider *yourself* warned."

It was Olivia's turn to laugh as he headed up the steps into the house. He paused at the doorway, turning back. "Oh, and if Samantha calls to check up on me—"

Olivia's stomach tightened. She did her best to keep her smile from becoming strained at the mention of the name.

"—Maybe don't mention that I came home early." John gave her a conspiratorial wink. "We'll keep that our little secret."

It was no effort now to grin back. Olivia nodded, crossing her heart and twisting the invisible key over her mouth again. "Secret's safe with me."

Miles was the first one to join her out back, Frisbee in hand. "Where's Dad?"

"Getting changed." Olivia motioned for him to toss it to her. "Let's get some practice in before he comes out. I may or may not have made some challenges that I need to back up . . ."

They settled into a good back-and-forth, until during one of the tosses, Miles abruptly fell to the ground, ignoring the Frisbee completely as it sailed past his head.

Olivia frowned, concerned. "Are you all right?"

He shook it off, rising back to his feet as he trotted after the Frisbee and tossed it back to her.

Still frowning, Olivia caught it and held onto it for a minute "Did you feel dizzy or something?"

Miles just shook his head again, seeming a little disoriented. "Throw it back to me!" he called, clapping his hands impatiently.

Olivia did; again, they tossed it back and forth a few times, and everything seemed normal, until abruptly Miles collapsed again.

Olivia rushed to his side, joined immediately by John. "What's going on? What happened to him?"

"I think he might have a serious neurological disorder," Cursing herself internally, Olivia wondered how she could have been so oblivious. She'd been one of the leading pediatric oncologists in the UK, and Miles had been under her watch and care day and night for the past three months. How could she have not seen the signs sooner?

John gaped at her. "What do you mean? He just fell down, it's not serious, and it doesn't mean anything—"

Olivia reached out to touch his arm, halting the flow of panicked words. "John, listen to me. I know this is going to sound crazy, but I know what I'm talking about. I . . ." She hesitated, knowing she still couldn't reveal too much about herself; but if ever there was a time to talk about her past, it was now. "I used to be a pediatric oncologist, before . . . everything. I've seen this a dozen times."

John's eyes darted back and forth between before, swallowing, he nodded. "What do we do?"

"We have to get him to a neurologist, and soon." Olivia racked her brain. "I wish I knew someone here in Florida. The closest I can think of is Madelina." "Madelina?"

"She's the head of neurology at the Children's Hospital in Boston, and an old colleague and friend." Olivia shook her head. "But Boston's so far, and we need to get him seen immediately . . ."

John shook his head, cutting off her protest. "We can take my jet. They're always on standby; if I call right now, they can be ready within the hour."

Olivia hesitated, but only for a moment; Miles's well being was of far greater importance than keeping her past buried. Nodding, she rose to her feet. "I'll call her right away . . ."

John caught her arm before she had gone two steps, his eyes earnest as they met her own. "Thank you, Melissa."

Nodding, Olivia slipped out of his grasp and raced toward the house.

Chapter Eighteen

Olivia paced the room nervously as the phone rang in her hands. She and Madelina Lopez had become close after meeting at a conference in Switzerland, and she knew if there was anyone in the world she could trust, it was she; still, how to explain everything that had happened, and the bizarre turn of events that had led her to become Melissa Spencer, Palm Beach governess?

The other end clicked as Madelina answered. "Dr. Lopez speaking."

"Madelina, hi. It's . . . Olivia Franklin."

"Olivia?" she could hear the astonishment in the other woman's voice. "Where on earth are you? The last I'd heard, you were a missing person, presumed dead . . ."

Olivia took in a sharp breath. None of this was news to her, but still, hearing it out loud made it seem somehow more real. "I know. It's a long story, and one that I promise to tell you in full, but right now I need your help . . ."

The house was a flurry of preparations as Olivia, John, and Janett worked to get everything ready for the trip. Madelina had been able to pull a few strings to schedule Miles in for as soon as they could arrive—with the understanding that Olivia would explain everything to her once she got there. Especially after Olivia had revealed to her that the people she was arriving with knew her only as Melissa Spencer, not Olivia Franklin.

"I'm worried about you, *m'ija*, but I trust you," Madelina had told her. "Now get yourself and that little boy out here as quickly and safely as you can."

As soon as she got off the line with Madelina, Olivia hurriedly dialed Fred to fill him in on the change in plans. " . . .We'll be leaving as soon as the jet is ready," she concluded as she stuffed a duffel bag full of Miles's clothes.

"I'm coming with you," Fred returned without any further preamble. "At least as far as the airport. Then I have a couple guys who can meet you in Boston and escort you to the hospital."

As soon as she finished with the call, Olivia raced down the stairs, bag in tow—only to come face-to-face with Samantha as she entered the house, carrying two bags of Chinese takeout. "Who's hungry?" she called brightly, until her eyes narrowed in on Olivia. "Oh. Melissa." Noticing the duffel bag, she visibly brightened. "Going somewhere?"

Olivia was saved the necessity of answering as John entered, carrying Miles in his arms. The boy was conscious now, which was a good sign, but still weak, and twitching every so often.

At the sight of Samantha, John stopped dead in his tracks. "What are you doing here?"

Samantha, to her credit, had gone pale at the sight of Miles. "What's going on? Is he all right . . .?" As quickly and tersely as he could, John filled her in on the details. Samantha set the food down on the counter, pulling out her phone. "Let me just have my assistant bring over a few things and I'll be ready to go."

John just stared at her, "You aren't coming with us."

Samantha froze, eyebrows rising as she gaped back at him. "Excuse me?" Sighing, John shook his head. "I didn't mean it like that, it's just . . . Time is of the essence. We should already be heading out to the airport now, and I don't even know if there'll be room—"

"We?" Samantha interrupted him, her voice quiet but her eyebrows so high that they nearly touched her hairline.

John exchanged a guilty glance with Olivia. "He's been asking for Melissa. They're so close—you have to understand . . ."

"Oh, I understand perfectly." And, snatching her keys from off the countertop, Samantha stormed out of the house.

In that instant John knew that he and Samantha were over. She did not understand how important Miles was to him and his feeling had changed dramatically in the past two months. John thought to himself, "When I get back, Samantha and I will have a very difficult conversation."

Back in the safety of her own car, Samantha slammed the door for good measure, fuming in silence for a few moments before she snatched out her phone and made a call. "Inspector Quinn? This is Samantha Emerson. I just thought you should know your girl is on the run. If you want to find Olivia Franklin, be at the Signature Terminal on Perimeter Road in twenty minutes." Swallowing, she couldn't help but add peevishly, "I wasn't invited."

Without waiting for a response, she hung up, tossing the phone into the passenger seat beside her.

On the other end of the line, R.W. Curran smiled to himself, hanging up his own mobile phone and slipping it back into his pocket.

Things were finally starting to look up.

Chapter Nineteen

Fred maneuvered his beat-up Impala through traffic, careful to hang back two or three cars behind John Verner's shiny Bentley. On paper, nothing could have made more sense than Olivia's unplanned excursion to Boston—Miles had symptoms of a brain tumor, and she had connections in Massachusetts that could very well save the boy's life. Still, something about the trip niggled him in the wrong way. There was danger lurking nearby, he just couldn't quite place his finger on what. And until he saw Olivia safely on the plane himself, he knew that feeling wouldn't be going away anytime soon.

"Come on," he groaned in irritation as an SUV pulled in front of him, cutting off his view of the Bentley. There were only a few more miles to the airport, so why did he feel like he was sitting on a ticking time bomb just waiting to go off?

In the darkened SUV just ahead of Fred Connors, R.W. Curran followed closely on the black Bentley's trail. He had Olivia Franklin in his sights. Now all he needed was some kind of distraction, some way that he could get easy access to the woman before she got on the plane, and end this relentless search once and for all.

Up ahead of him, the cars slowed to a crawl and then stopped altogether as they reached the edge of the Royal Palm Drawbridge, positioned over the Intracoastal Waterway, which at the moment was beginning the long, tedious process of raising to allow the passage of ships underneath, causing a lengthy roadblock in the meantime.

From behind his darkened sunglasses, Curran grinned.

"Seriously?" Fred grumbled to himself as the brake lights of the SUV in front of him glared red. Up ahead of him, a line of cars ground to a halt, and he reluctantly followed suit with the Impala, tapping his fingers restlessly on the steering wheel. "Come on, come on."

In the SUV ahead of him, the driver's door opened and a man stepped out. Some impatient guy who thought it was his job to walk to the front of the traffic jam and see what was going on—Fred knew his type well.

Then the man paused, glancing over his shoulder to search the bridge around him.

It took Fred less than a second to recognize that face even disguised as it was underneath a baseball cap and dark sunglasses.

R.W. Curran—

—Who was reaching into his coat and pulling out a concealed weapon.

"No!" Fumbling to put the Impala into park, Fred scrambled to reach his own weapon, stored in his glove compartment.

It took him approximately five seconds to find it, but by then it was already too late.

Approaching the passenger side of the Bentley, Curran angled his gun downward and fired.

The first bullet shattered the glass. Curran fired two more for good measure, at approximately the height where he knew Olivia Franklin's head would be. It was a good, clean kill, and she wouldn't suffer; he had nothing personal against the woman, after all. He was simply doing his duty.

In the car behind him, a man was scrambling out of the driver's side, gun raised. Undercover police by the looks of him; Olivia had been smart to have someone like that on her trail.

But not smart enough.

The man fired, narrowly missing Curran's head as he ducked back. It was time to make a clean escape, but first he would spare a few seconds to ensure the job was complete so he could report back on it with authority to his superiors.

Screams and shouts of dismay echoed from within the car beyond Olivia Franklin's blood-soaked corpse, bits of brain and skin splattered across the roof of the vehicle. At last, it was over. Nodding grimly to himself, Curran had just turned to go—

—When out of the corner of his eye, he spotted Olivia Franklin.

Sitting in the back seat, hugging a frantic Miles Verner to her side.

Alive and well.

He pieced it together in an instant. John Verner must have changed his mind and allowed his fiancé to come along. Samantha Emerson, whose phone call tipping off Curran's location to Olivia Franklin might very well have been her last?

It was a regrettable casualty, but not too late to be fixed. Curran raised his gun again, aiming for Olivia, who pushed the screaming boy away from her, trying to shield him from the attack.

Another gunshot rang out—but not from Curran's gun. The undercover cop was gaining on him; the bullet fired so close to its mark that Curran had actually felt it whizzing past his ear.

He'd been so close. *She'd* been so close. Casting one last regretful glance at Olivia, he turned, hoisting himself over the railing, before dropping into the water beneath.

Chapter Twenty

As police and ambulance crews swarmed the scene, a stunned John Verner sat wrapped on the tailgate of an ambulance, trying to focus as the police officers asked him yet another round of questions.

Samantha.

She was dead.

He'd killed her right in front of their eyes.

Blinking and attempting to force his way out of the shock, Verner interrupted the latest line of interrogation, clutching at the sleeve of the officer. "My son. He has a brain tumor. We need to get him to Boston as soon as possible—the plane is waiting." The officer—who'd up until this point looked nothing but stern and no-nonsense—softened into some semblance of humanity. "I'm sympathetic to that, Mr. Verner, I really am. But we have an investigation we're trying to run." John refused to lessen his grip on the man, holding his gaze. "Please. It's my son."

As the officer showed signs of wavering, another voice interrupted the conversation, stepping in. "Maybe I can help."

John looked up in surprise to see a vaguely familiar face approaching. It took him a second to place him as Fred Connors, the man Melissa had snuck off to meet that one afternoon that now seemed so long ago. At the time, the man had set his blood boiling, though John hardly understood why; now he felt almost shaky with relief at the familiar face.

"Detective Fred Connors," he introduced himself to the officer, flashing his badge. "I think I can be of some assistance. I was in the vehicle behind the perpetrator and saw the entire thing. I'm sure you've seen the bulletins for the international terrorist, R.W. Curran? He was the one behind this attack—I've been following this investigation for some time . . ."

Was that why the man had pulled Melissa away from work that day? John felt briefly guilty for his overreaction, until a new thought struck him. He'd assumed that Samantha's death had been part of some random carjacking, but if Fred had been trailing the man for some time, and had purposefully come by to track down Melissa—then was she somehow connected to all of this?

The officer shook his head ruefully. "Unfortunately, we can't just let all of our witnesses hop on a plane and leave the state. It's protocol."

"No, yeah, of course." Fred brooded over it briefly, rubbing at the back of his neck. "What if you kept Mr. Verner and me here for questioning, and let the boy go with his governess to Boston to keep his appointment?"

He met John's gaze briefly, seeming to be willing him to comply. John hesitated. If Melissa was somehow connected to this dangerous man who had just killed his fiancé, he didn't especially want to send off his son with her—besides which, he acknowledged to himself with a painful tightening of his gut, he couldn't bear the thought of letting her out of his sight if she was in danger.

But at the same time, Melissa was the one with connections in Boston, and Miles needed to get help right away. And maybe it would be best to get her out of the state where that madman would have less of a chance of reaching her—which was probably why Fred Connors was so eager to get her on that plane.

Still conflicted, John nonetheless felt himself nodding in agreement. "We can handle it on this end," he assured the officer. "Just let my son get the help he needs."

Olivia provided the officer with a brief audio statement recorded in the police officer's phone. Olivia didn't have much information. She didn't know the man who shot Samantha and she had no idea that she was the killer's target.

Chapter Twenty-One

After a long and anxious flight, Olivia and Miles were met at the airport by Detective Tanveer Paleti, a tall, handsome Indian man and a close friend of Fred's, who escorted them in a squad car to the Children's Hospital.

Madelina Lopez was waiting for them at the front entrance, her face a mask of concern as she took in Olivia's altered appearance. Olivia could see the dozens upon dozens of questions forming on the other woman's lips—but, ever the consummate professional, she instructed the nurse at her side to get Miles into a wheelchair so they could start him on the necessary series of tests. "Melissa, Miles's father faxed to me power of attorney authorizing Melissa Spenser to make all medical decisions on Miles's behalf, so we can get started," Madelina said.

"Hello, Miles," Madelina said in her usual cool, calm manner. It was her practice not to speak down to children but to treat them with the same compassion and understanding she would adult patients, and the result was that the children most often felt inspired by her confidence in them to rise to the task at hand. "I've heard you're a very brave young man. Are you ready to be brave tonight?"

Miles held her gaze solemnly, nodding his head.

Madelina squeezed his hand. "Good. Then we can both be brave, together."

A few hours later, after what felt like dozens upon dozens of tests, Miles was checked into a room as they waited for the results to come in. He'd been a virtual adventurer-lion-tamer-astronaut-fireman all rolled into one, not crying or screaming or showing any signs of fear. It wasn't until he was alone with Olivia, realizing that he was going to be staying in the hospital overnight, that he showed his only sign of weakness, reaching over to squeeze her arm.

"Don't leave me by myself, Melissa," he whispered.

Olivia fought back the tears that threatened to show. It was her turn to be brave now. "Never," she vowed to him, kissing his forehead tenderly.

She had a cot brought into Miles's room so she could stay the night by his side. It had been an eventful day, in more ways than one, and it didn't take long for the boy to fall into a deep sleep.

Olivia was not so fortunate. Her mind raced with the events of the day. Curran's approach on the bridge, Samantha's snide smile as she turned back to face Olivia, opening her mouth to speak—before suddenly bullets pierced the glass, forever silencing whatever the other woman had been about to say.

On the bed beside her, Miles twitched as if he could sense her own disquiet. The poor boy had been through so much already—witnessing his mother's death, and now Samantha's. And to top it all off, it was more than likely that he'd have to battle his way through a brain tumor, too. It wasn't fair; none of it was fair. Even though Olivia logically knew that she had nothing to do with Julia's death or Miles's possible cancer, a tired, irrational part of her could not help but feel responsible. She was poison to all of the people around her.

Like her parents, who had been blown up inside of their own home as a desperate attempt to cover her true lineage.

And Daniel, shot and killed before her very eyes.

Even Diana, who'd died in such a senseless, tragic way before Olivia had ever even gotten the chance to truly know her.

Tears now staining her pillowcase, Olivia did her best to muffle her sobs, not wanting to wake the boy sleeping on the bed next to her. At least there was still a chance with him. If it were too late, if she hadn't caught the signs early enough, she would never forgive herself. Especially because she knew how much it would devastate John.

John Verner. The man who'd seemed so aloof and cold to her at first, who had slowly thawed before her eyes into a kind, complicated man with demons of his own hanging over his shoulder. In many ways, he was so different from Daniel—and yet in so many ways, they were the same. Their strength. Their bravery. Their intelligence. Their kindness.

It didn't seem like she'd ever actually fallen asleep, but suddenly she woke up to find John sitting in a chair beside the bed, as if he'd been there all night, though Olivia hadn't noticed his arrival. Despite his awkward position, he was deep in sleep, the lines of his face furrowed into a harsh frown. Every so often, his hand twitched on his knee, but otherwise he was lost to the world of dreams.

Olivia rolled over, watching him for a long, soundless moment. Suddenly, inexplicably, she knew.

She loved him.

Somehow, slowly but surely, John Verner had wormed his way into her heart. After Daniel, she hadn't thought it was still possible to feel that way again, but she couldn't deny her attraction to John, or the way he seemed to warm her from the inside out. Sometimes she could even convince herself that he might feel the same way . . .

But was it Melissa Spencer that he truly loved? What would happen when he finally got to know Olivia Franklin?

Sighing as she fought back a fresh wave of tears, Olivia turned her back to John, pressing her eyes shut and willing sleep to overtake her once more.

Charles nervously scrolled through the images on his mobile phone of the attack which had taken place earlier that day in the States. The traffic on the bridge, the seemingly random attack from known terrorist R.W. Curran on an unsuspecting woman. Some of the more graphic photographs showed the woman, whom Curran must have mistaken for Olivia. She hardly looked human anymore, her skull nothing but bits of bone and bloody clumps of hair in some places.

Of course he'd known this was what he had instigated when he'd put out the order for Olivia's life, but it was a different matter, seeing the aftermath for himself. Having served in the Royal Navy, he was no stranger to violence and bloodshed, but this…this felt different.

Charles paused on one of the photographs, squinting, then zoomed in as best as he was able. Yes, just as he'd suspected—in the background of one, blurry but unmistakable, was Olivia. She'd dyed her hair and looked to be wearing some colored contacts to disguise herself, but the bone structure and bearing was distinct.

Olivia. His daughter, at least biologically. She'd become something of a boogeyman in his mind, but here she did not look so intimidating, only frightened.

Swallowing, Charles switched over to his secured phone and dialed Curran's number. He was relieved but unsurprised when it went straight to voicemail—he assumed being on the run from the United States government after what was being considered an international terrorist attack must take up some time.

"Curran, it's me." No need to identify himself, and furthermore, for security reasons it was better not to do so. "I know what we discussed earlier, but I… I've changed my mind. I want her alive."

He ended the call, slipping the mobile back into his pocket. What to do with her once he had her was a different matter, but he would deal with it then. *Later.*

And, if he was being honest with himself, a part of him hoped it would be *never.*

Chapter Twenty-Two

Breakfast, Olivia had promised Madelina during the rush of the previous evening. Eggs, pancakes, coffee, and a huge heaping dose of the truth.

But now as Olivia sat opposite her old friend at the hospital cafeteria table, not only did she have no stomach for the food heaped before her, but also no words to describe the journey she had been through that had brought her to this place.

Seeming to understand her reticence, Madelina gave her a sympathetic smile, reaching out to squeeze her hand. "Why don't you just start from the beginning?"

So, Olivia did. She told Madelina everything—the attack in the hospital. Philip Churchill, trying so desperately to cover up the truth about her birth that he inadvertently set her on the path to discovering her real biological parents: Princess Diana and Prince Charles. Reuniting with Daniel after being apart for so long. The murder of her parents. Going on the run with Daniel across Europe. Stopping Churchill, but knowing all the while that it wasn't over yet. Fleeing to Africa, being so happy there working with the children, and falling into the trap of believing she was safe. Daniel's murder, and coming to live in the States undercover—not as Olivia Franklin, but as Melissa Spencer.

Madelina listened in silence until Olivia was finished before reaching out to give her hand another sympathetic squeeze. "It sounds like you've been to hell and back, my friend."

Olivia nodded in grim confirmation. "And back to hell again. John has no idea who I am, and just how much I've put his family in danger. And now Miles . . . I honestly don't know what I'd do if anything happened to him."

They were interrupted as a nurse approached Madelina, grim-faced. "Dr. Lopez? The results have come in for Miles Verner . . ."

Meeting Madelina's gaze, Olivia took in a deep breath, steeling herself.

"As you thought Olivia, Miles does have a brain tumor, more specifically, Cerebellar Astrocytoma. Thankfully it is benign but it must be removed quickly." Madelina said with great relief in her voice. "The tests indicate that the tumor has not progressed to the brainstem so we do not anticipate the need for radiation therapy or chemotherapy. I had asked my colleagues, neurosurgeon, Dr. Henry Pong and Dr. James Clancy, Neurosurgeon-in-Chief to review the results and they concur."

Although the diagnosis appeared to be good, immediate surgery would be necessary.

Madelina explained to John upon his arrival Miles's diagnosis and her plan for his surgery.

A grim faced John Verner watched the nursing staff prep his son. Just as they were readying to wheel him off to the operating room, John stepped in, gathering Miles into his arms and holding him as if he'd never let him go. Inwardly, he cursed himself for all the missed time, for those years he'd been present physically but so distant mentally and emotionally, wallowing in Julia's death when his son was still alive and needed him so much. He would never make that mistake again, if given a second chance. He would never waste a single moment.

"I love you, Miles," he murmured over and over again, at a loss for any other words but needing his son to know that much, "I love you, I love you, I love you . . ."

After a minute or so of this, Miles began to squirm. "It's okay, Dad. I'm brave."

Despite himself, John laughed, releasing his hold on Miles so he could settle himself back down onto the gurney. "I know you are, my boy. I'll see you when you're done."

He stepped back, hoping that Miles hadn't noticed the tears springing up in his eyes. His boy was being so courageous; it was time that John stepped up to the plate and did the same.

Melissa moved in after him, bending down low to kiss Miles's forehead before wrapping him in an embrace of her own. "See you on the other side, Little Monkey," she murmured into his ear. "I love you."

"Love you, too, Melissa."

Watching them together, John felt an unexpected jolt of realization. He loved her. It was perhaps the worst time and the worst place to realize it, but he loved Melissa, and had for quite some time now. Slowly but surely she had managed to heal their family and bring them back together again. And he could not fathom any kind of happiness, without her and Miles there beside him.

"It's time to go," one of the orderlies spoke up, gentle but firm.

Releasing Miles, Melissa stepped back beside John, and the two of them watched together as the nurses wheeled Miles down the hallway, trying their best to smile until he was out of sight.

Chapter Twenty-Three

They waited.

And waited.

And waited.

Not all that much time had passed, and yet it seemed like a lifetime. Olivia was going mad, cooped up on the plastic waiting-room chairs, trying to read a two-year-old magazine or watch the television, but unable to focus on anything except for the constant, raging fear.

She'd thought she'd done a fairly good job covering all this up until John abruptly reached over and took her hand. No doubt, sensing her nerves—or perhaps, overcome with nerves of his own. Regardless, Olivia was thankful for the comfort, and laced her fingers through his, squeezing back.

After what seemed like an eternity, Madelina finally approached them from down the hall, still scrubbed out from the surgery. Olivia felt her stomach plummet. Exchanging a glance with John—and seeing her own terror mirrored back at her from his eyes—they stood together, hands still entwined, as they waited.

Drawing nearer, Madelina gave a weary smile and nodded. "It couldn't have gone more perfectly," she reassured them. "We'll have to hold him for observation and run a few more tests to be positive, but from what I've seen today, I feel confident that we were able to remove all of the tumor and his recovery should be textbook."

The relief caused Olivia's legs to nearly buckle underneath her. Luckily, John was there to hold her up. He enveloped her in his arms, holding her so tightly that Olivia thought he might never let her go. And a part of her never wanted him to, either.

Eddie Armstrong stepped out onto the curb at Logan Airport, stretching up his arms until his back gave a loud, satisfying pop. It had been a long flight but well worth it; now he would finally be able to see Olivia again and know for himself that she was safe, just as he had promised Daniel he would do.

Scarcely had he taken two steps onto American soil before a car door opened and a man in a leather jacket with buzzed hair stepped out of his car. "Eddie Armstrong?"

Eddie took in the sight of the man he'd previously only contacted through phone conversations. "Fred Connors?"

"Nice to meet you, man." Fred shook his hand, motioning him toward the car. "Why don't we get you to the hospital? I'm sure Olivia can't wait to see you."

This was confirmed at the hospital, where Olivia rushed out into the lobby to greet him, throwing her into his arms. Eddie held onto her tightly. It was one thing to exchange phone calls and e-mails but quite another to see for himself that she was alive and healthy and well. For both of them, seeing the other was as close to being with Daniel as they could ever hope to get; but it was more than that, too. They had survived something together, virtually been to war together, and Eddie would do everything in his power to see that Olivia got her happily ever after.

"Hey, kiddo." He pulled back, bucking her chin affectionately. "Aren't they feeding you here?"

Olivia smiled, shrugging her shoulders. "American food. You know how it is."

Eddie grimaced sympathetically. "Not a Cornish pasty to be found, eh?"

"Hey!" Fred spoke up from behind them in mock offense. "Ever heard of a hamburger before? Those things are pretty damn good."

Olivia broke away from Eddie to hug Fred, then back to Eddie one more time. "I'm so glad you're here." She pulled away, raising a stern eyebrow at Eddie. "But are you sure you can take so much leave off work?"

Eddie exchanged a glance with Fred; they'd discussed this on the car ride over here. "Truth be told, I'm taking a little break from Scotland Yard." At the protest he could already see forming on Olivia's lips, he held up his hands, "Only until we can get Curran behind bars. And don't give me that look—my job will be *fine*. They can't live without me over there, trust me."

Before Olivia could protest the matter any further, John stepped out into the hallway, seeming to have recognized his brother-in-law's voice. Seeing Eddie, John stepped in, enveloping him in an uncharacteristic hug. Bloody hell. Maybe they couldn't live without him over here, either.

"How's the kid?" Eddie asked as soon as they broke apart.

"Doing really well," John returned, "and recovering just as quickly as they'd hoped. There's even talk that we might be able to check him out of here in the next couple of days."

"That's great!" Eddie said, and meant it. Although he got to spend very little time with his nephew, the kid held a special place in his heart—he looked so much like Julia, after all.

John's smile faded into a frown of confusion as he noticed Fred Connors standing just beyond Eddie. Damn. Eddie had forgotten that John had already met Fred and knew he was a detective. Now he would be doubtlessly piecing together the fact that Fred and Eddie seemed to be working together, and that both apparently had ties to Olivia . . .

"So what brings you to town, Eddie?"

Eddie thought quickly. "Well, Olivia filled me in on everything that's been happening with Miles, and when she found out her friend Fred was going to be coming back to Boston, she arranged for him to pick me up at the airport so I could come in and check up on the kid."

It was a plausible enough story, so it surprised Eddie when John's frown only deepened. "Who's Olivia?"

Whoops. Bloody jetlag, he was totally off his game today. "Did I say Olivia?" He forced a laugh, shaking his head as he rubbed the bridge of his nose. "Think the time change must be wearing off on me. I meant Melissa, of course. Sorry, luv." He glanced to Fred. "Do you think you could drop me by my hotel, mate?"

Fred played along. "Sure thing."

John seemed to have bought it. "Well, I should get back to Miles. Go get some sleep and then come visit him, okay? I'm sure he'd be thrilled to see you."

"Will do." Eddie waited until John had left the hallway before turning back to the other two. "Sorry. I'm a bloody idiot."

"I think John's starting to put things together," Fred observed. "Do you really think it would be the worst idea in the world to fill him in on a few things? Poor guy's been through enough; he deserves to know that his family might be in danger."

Eddie glanced back at Olivia, gauging her reaction. To his surprise, she looked pale-faced, stricken, as though her heart was near to bursting from her chest. *Ah*, Eddie understood all at once. *So that's how it is.*

"Olivia?" he prompted gently after a moment.

Olivia blinked, coming back to them. "I want to tell him," she murmured, "I just . . . I don't know how."

Eddie reached out, taking her hand. "Take some time, luv. But not *too* much time. It will be best, coming from you."

Olivia nodded her head but bit down on her lip, heart still seeming torn.

It wouldn't be an easy thing, Eddie mused, telling the man you loved that you'd been lying to him all this time.

Chapter Twenty-Four

John popped his head back out into the hallway to see that Fred Connors and Eddie had left, but Melissa still stood in the hallway, staring off into space. "Melissa?"

She started, whirling back to face him. "John, you startled me."

He offered a wry smile. "I can see that. Is everything okay?"

Melissa smiled back at him, thought something about it seemed strained, forced. "Of course. Just worried about Miles, that's all."

John hesitated, wondering if he should press further. He knew Melissa really was concerned about Miles; it was obvious that the two absolutely adored each other. But he wondered if her stress didn't have something more to do with Eddie showing up suddenly in Boston. He wondered if something new had happened with her domestic dispute case. But then, it seemed a bit strange to him that there should be so much secrecy and intrigue about a husband beating his wife. Was it possible that Olivia's husband had been involved in something political? Had maybe even been a terrorist?

Okay, so perhaps his imagination was getting a bit ahead of him. Besides which, that was Melissa's business, not his own, and she would talk to him about it when and if she needed to. Until then, he needed to respect her space. "I was just wondering if I could borrow your iPad really quick and check on something for work?"

Melissa seemed relieved at the response; had she been expecting a more pressing question from him? Perhaps something to do with her past?

Snap out of it, Verner, John warned himself again. He was respecting her, dammit.

"Sure. It's in my leather satchel by the bed in Miles's room."

John thanked her with a parting smile and slipped back inside. Miles was sleeping again—which was good, the doctors reassured him. His body needed time to rebuild all of its old strength. In the meantime, he found Melissa's bag and the iPad inside, settling down into the chair beside the bed as he clicked it on.

As the screen warmed up, he realized he was in Melissa's library. He was just about to flip out to find an Internet browser when a title caught his eye—*The Disappearance of Olivia*. Olivia. Wasn't that the name that Eddie had accidentally called Melissa out in the hallway?

Intrigued, John clicked on the title, merely intending to scan through the first few pages.

Forty-five minutes later, he was a good chunk of the way through the book and could not help but notice some of the uncanny similarities between the title character—Olivia Franklin—and his own Melissa Spencer. Both British, both pediatric oncologists forced to go on the run. And hadn't he heard Melissa say something about a 'Daniel' before? Not to mention the fact that Eddie Armstrong was one of the main characters of the book . . .

But there was the striking difference that Olivia was supposed to be blond-haired and blue-eyed, and Melissa had dark hair and brown eyes. Not to mention the fact that Olivia Franklin was supposed to be Princess Diana's biological daughter, obviously making it a piece of fiction and nothing more.

Right?

Before John could ponder on it too long, he heard the sound of approaching footsteps and quickly switched the browser over to the Internet, scanning through his e-mails, as he'd originally intended to do.

The door opened, and Melissa poked her head inside. "I was going to grab some dinner. Would you like anything?"

"I'm all right," John reassured her, smiling as he watched her go.

Melissa Spencer.

The woman he'd been getting to know over the past few months.

The woman he'd been falling in love with.

. . . Right?

Chapter Twenty-Five

Two weeks later . . .

"Is that it?" an excited Miles asked, pointing out the window of their hotel room in the Four Seasons.

John crossed over to join him, pushing back the curtain. Now that the worst of the initial surgeries and treatments was over and Miles was well on his way to recovery, he was enjoying having the time off to play endless games, watch as much TV as he liked—and be on the constant lookout for snow. A Florida boy through and through, he had never glimpsed the cold white precipitation for himself, and more often than not, he could be found at the window, searching.

"Sorry to disappoint," John returned, biting back a smile, "but that's sleet. Close, but no cigar."

Miles groaned, falling back against the bed. "When I'm going to get to see snow?"

Kids were so remarkably resilient that way. Miles had undergone surgery, been hooked up to an IV, had to scarf down nothing but hospital food for weeks, and he'd done all of that without complaint; but deprive him of the right to see the snow, and suddenly it was the end of the world.

Biting back a laugh, John leaned down to kiss the top of Miles's head, carefully so as not to upset any of the bandages. "Well, it is Boston in the wintertime. You just might be in luck, sooner or later." He picked up a

Hardy Boys book—which had quickly become one of Miles's favorites once he'd learned it used to be John's favorite as a boy. "Want me to read to you some more?"

At Miles's enthusiastic nod, John settled himself on the bed beside his son, falling quickly into the rhythm of the words. But in truth, his mind was far away—in particular, on Melissa. As the adrenaline of the past few days had finally died down, he'd begun to wonder if some of his feelings hadn't been heightened by the stress of Miles's tumor and the shooting on the bridge.

But as time went on, he soon found that his feelings were only deepening with each passing day. It hadn't just been the stress or the chaos. He loved Melissa Spenser, and he wanted to spend the rest of his life with her.

A part of him couldn't help but feel guilty—the usual, residual guilt over being able to love anyone else now that Julia was gone, added to a new guilt after Samantha's death. With some distance, he could see that Samantha hadn't been the best choice, one made in the grief of Julia's passing and in the desperation to numb the pain and find a new mother for Miles. That wasn't to say that he wasn't horrified about what had happened to her, or sad that she was gone. But he could see now that she had never been right for him.

He'd assumed after Julia's death that it was normal that he would never feel even half of what he'd felt for her with another woman, but Melissa had made him realize that just wasn't true. He loved her. He needed her. And he was desperate to be with her.

Glancing down, John saw that Miles had been lulled into a deep, untroubled sleep. He set down the book on the bedside table, carefully extracting himself so that his son could get some much-needed rest. He would just slip off for a minute down the hall to get some more ice.

Outside the room door, the unexpected but extremely pleasant sight of Melissa, sneaking out of her own room, just across the hall, greeted him. At the sight of him, she froze, a guilty smile stretching across her face.

John raised an eyebrow at her. "I thought we agreed you were going to take the afternoon off and take a much-needed nap."

"I was. I *am*." Melissa wrung her hands in front of her, adorably flustered. "I just wanted to make sure that you knew where Miles's new prescription was, just in case he needed it—"

"Melissa." John surprised himself by placing a finger against her soft lips, silencing her. "Miles is fine. He's resting. You've been with him around the clock, which I appreciate more than you'll ever know, but it's time for you to get some rest, too."

Melissa's eyes darted down to his finger. She swallowed before meeting his gaze, nodding.

"Promise me?" John pressed as she began to back away toward her own room.

The grin she flashed him sent a sharp pang of longing through his gut. "Promise."

"Melissa?"

Loathe letting her out of his sight, even for a second, her name had escaped his mouth before he could stop himself. She stopped, turning back, her eyebrows raised in a question, and John searched for the right words. "Eddie is coming over to spend some uncle time with Miles tonight. So I was wondering if maybe . . .you'd let me fix you dinner?"

His heart was racing and his palms were sweating as profusely as if he was some clumsy teenage boy doing this for the first time. Melissa blinked at him in surprise, and for a moment he truly thought she might refuse him. Then she gave a slow, sweet smile. "I'd like that."

Like an idiot, John grinned back at her. "Okay. 8:00?"

"That would be lovely."

For an instant they lingered. Maybe it was only John's wishful thinking, but he thought maybe Melissa didn't want to leave his sight, either. Or maybe she was just disturbed by how he was grinning and staring at her.

Clearing his throat, John motioned to the bucket in his hand. "Ice!" he said more cheerfully than was necessary, giving a little half-wave as he moved down the hall.

Ice? He mouthed to himself as soon as he was out of sight, shaking his head to himself. What a moron.

In her own room, back pressed to the door, Olivia grinned to herself, running the pad of her thumb over the spot on her lips where John had touched her. If she wasn't mistaken, he had just asked her out on a date.

It was about bloody time.

As she tossed and turned in bed, attempting to take the nap that John had made her promise to take, she couldn't help but think it was a bit cruel of him to order her to sleep and then present her with an invitation that would guarantee that rest would be an impossibility. Finally after forty-five minutes of staring at the ceiling, she got up and drew herself a bath.

As Olivia soaped and shaved and scrubbed and lotioned, she could not shake the strangeness of the sensation. She was getting ready for a man. It had been such a long time. She wondered if she even still knew how to behave on a first date, if it would be like riding a bicycle and all come back to her in bits and pieces, or if she would be gawping and floundering at the table as John realized he'd made a terrible mistake in asking her. And yet—

She loved him. And if her intuition was correct, he loved her, too.

You mean, he loves Melissa Spencer, an ugly little voice in her head reminded her.

The thought sobered Olivia instantly, wiping the smile from her face. She and Melissa were one and the same, and yet . . .they weren't. Once John realized just how much she'd been keeping from him, would he still be able to look at her the same way, like he couldn't believe just how lucky he was that he'd found her?

Taking in a deep breath, Olivia abruptly plunged her head underwater, trying to purge the doubts from her mind.

It didn't work.

Chapter Twenty-Six

At eight o'clock sharp, someone knocked on the door. Olivia smiled to herself, taking one last look in the mirror. She'd tried on at least half a dozen dresses on Newbury Street before deciding on a simple yet elegant black cocktail dress. There was no way to go wrong in a little black dress, after all, and the effect was chic and sexy, if she did say so herself. Hopefully it would be enough to cause John's jaw to drop the moment he laid eyes on her.

However, it wasn't John at the door, but one of the hotel valets—though, gratifyingly, his mouth did hang open a bit at the sight of her. "M-miss Spencer?"

"Yes?" Her stomach plummeted with the sudden certainty that John had changed his mind and sent this boy to cancel for him.

"Mr. Verner asked me to escort you to the fifth floor."

Olivia frowned at this but obediently followed the valet down the hallway. The fifth floor? Then it clicked into place. If Eddie was going to be spending time with Miles in their suite, then John had probably rented out another so that they could have some time alone.

The thought both pleased and terrified her. All alone, in a beautiful hotel room overlooking the Boston Gardens, with John Verner. A man she would have sworn a month ago that she couldn't stand, and whom she now could not imagine her life without.

A man who had no idea who she truly was.

They soon reached the fifth floor. The valet led her to the suite marked 515, knocked, then gave her a crisp, oddly formal bow before walking away. Olivia bit back a smile as she watched him, shaking her head to herself. She hoped John tipped him well for that little performance.

"Come in!" came a muffled voice from inside the room.

Taking in a deep breath to steel her nerves, Olivia entered the room.

She didn't know quite what she'd been expecting, but none of it came anywhere close to what she saw before her. The room was filled bursting with roses, and Adele's low, sultry voice echoed through the sound-system—her favorite artist, though she didn't know how John could have possibly figured that out. In the middle of the room was a beautifully set table, draped in elegant linens and adorned with silver, crystal, and candles.

Navigating her way into the room, Olivia's gaze caught on the sofa, and she did a double take as she saw a Cartier box sitting on top of four Neiman Marcus boxes. Now it was her turn for her jaw to drop open. She knew John was wealthy, but still she'd been expecting a nice dinner and a good bottle of wine. This by far surpassed anything she'd imagined.

Searching the room, she at last found John, standing in the corner, gauging her reaction. Meeting her gaze, he gave a sheepish shrug of his shoulders. "I'm American, remember? We like to do things big."

Olivia shook her head, finally managing to find her voice. "You really do go all out for a first date, don't you?"

"Well." Another embarrassed shrug. "It *is* Valentine's Day."

Frowning, Olivia raced through the calendar in her mind. With everything that had happened, she'd forgotten entirely, but John was right. It was indeed the 14th of February. Looking up, she caught a glimmer of nervousness in his eyes and beamed at him to let him know she approved. "Can't wait to see what you put together for St. Patrick's Day," she quipped.

He grinned back at her. "Let's just say it involves some Irish whiskey and a bathtub full of four-leaf clovers—but I can't say anything more, it would ruin the surprise."

Olivia laughed. "I can't wait."

For a second longer, they stood, just smiling at one another. Then John stepped forward, swallowing as he reached for her hand; and, swallowing, Olivia gave it to him, allowing him to escort her to the table.

They talked about anything and everything—favorite books, favorite films, favorite music, and childhood memories. Fears, and embarrassing moments, both shared and independent of one another. Dreams and hopes for the future.

It was perfect. Even more so than the flowers and the music and the jewelry—which was all lovely, overwhelmingly so—she wouldn't have traded anything for this opportunity to get to know John, the actuality, not just John as she'd imagined him. He told her about building his business up from nothing, about meeting and falling in love with Julia, about holding Miles in his arms for the first time. About the vow he'd made that Miles would know his father in a way that John never had.

It was beautiful, and perfect . . . and bittersweet. Because as much as Olivia loved knowing all about John's past, each time it hit her with a renewed pang that she could not do the same with him. That as much as she enjoyed telling him about her literary love affair with the fictional Mr. Darcy, rivaled only by her adoration for white chocolate, she still couldn't tell him any real facts about herself. Nothing about her parents, nothing about her background. She couldn't even tell him Daniel's last name—or her own true name, for that matter.

She knew that John was trying his best to understand. Eddie had informed him from the very beginning that "Melissa" wouldn't be able to tell him anything from her past, and she could see that he was trying to be a gentleman about it and steer clear of topics he knew she could not answer. But it must be so frustrating, to reveal so much of yourself and to receive so little in return.

I have to tell him.

The thought had crossed Olivia's mind before, but never so calmly, and never so assuredly. Yet, as soon as she thought the words, she knew they were right. Surely, if there was anyone she could trust in the entire world, it was John Verner. And she wanted—no, *needed*, for him to know who she really was.

Still, even with this certainty, Olivia's mouth ran dry at the prospect. She took a sip of her wine before pressing her palms flat onto the table. "John? There's something I'd like to tell you."

John's smile faded ever so slightly, replaced by a look of grim certainty. She could tell he had been waiting for this moment almost as much as she had. Smiling, he reached out and took one of her hands. "All right."

"I . . ." Olivia swallowed, where to begin? She searched her mind, trying again. "I'm not who you think—"

A knock on the door interrupted them. Olivia was so startled she nearly knocked over her wine glass. That, coupled with her nerves, sent her into a gale of uncharacteristic giggles. "My goodness, that nearly gave me a heart attack."

John grinned back at her—both disappointed and relieved at once, it seemed. "Must be room service with our dessert. I'll be right back."

Olivia listened to the sound of him moving into the other room, taking in a deep breath to steady herself. Rising to her feet, she crossed over to the window, finding her center again as she looked out across the beautiful snow in the garden. She could do this. It wouldn't change anything, not really. It was Olivia Franklin he had fallen in love with, he just didn't know it yet.

The sound of a thump from the other room startled her back into the moment. Olivia frowned, taking a step toward the door. "John . . .?"

Strong hands gripped her from behind, closing around her neck. She screamed, trying to struggle away, but then felt a sharp, familiar prick in her neck and succumbed to the blackness.

Chapter Twenty-Seven

Darkness. A sharp agonizing throb in his temple. John groaned and struggled to sit up but was immediately forced to lie back down as the world swam up around him. He laid on the ground, breathing in heavily, eyes closed. There was something wet and sticky on the side of his face. He reached up, wiping it off with the back of his hand, then started as he opened his eyes and realized it was blood.

It all came rushing back to him at once. A severe blow to the back of his head. Lying on the ground, consciousness slipping away from him. The sounds of Melissa screaming in the other room.

He had to help her.

Struggling through the pain and the dizziness, John crawled forward on his elbows until finally he reached the bedside stand. Fumbling with bloodstained hands, he finally managed to get hold of the phone and pressed the button for guest services.

"Help me," he croaked into the receiver. "Help me . . ." And then the world slipped away from him once more.

Fred Connors pushed his way down the emergency room corridor, flashing his badge at anyone who put up a fuss. He'd meant to stop at the nurse's desk to ask where he could find John Verner, but instead all he had to do was follow the shouts.

"Miles! Miles!"

Turning one last corner, he found John Verner in the process of being strapped down to a gurney. The man's head was drenched in blood and he looked like he could barely keep his eyes open, and yet somehow he was still managing to thrash around enough that four on-call nurses had been summoned to help strap him down. "Miles!" Fred approached, using his best authoritative cop voice. "John, it's okay. It's okay. Miles is safe. He's back at the hotel with one of my sergeants. Eddie is on his way here now."

It was difficult to know how much of that John actually understood, since his eyes were still rolling about his head. At least he stopped bucking and thrashing, though he abruptly reached out, grabbing Fred's arm with his blood-soaked hand.

"Where is Melissa?" he rasped.

Fred shook his head, swallowing. "I don't know, John. I don't know."

By the time Eddie arrived, John's face had been cleaned up, his head bandaged, though the hospital was holding him while they waited for CT scan results before giving him the all-clear. At the sight of his approaching brother-in-law, John gripped the sides of his chair in anticipation. "Have they found Melissa?"

Eddie braced himself as he took the chair opposite. Walking into the hotel room had been like revisiting an old recurring nightmare. Furniture overturned. Blood staining the carpet. The window shattered. And worst of all, Olivia gone. He had sworn to her that he would keep this from ever happening to her again, and he had failed.

"Not yet." Eddie held John's gaze to let him know he wasn't just saying the things he thought John wanted to hear, treating him like a cop. "But I won't stop until we find her. You have my word."

John groaned, burying his face in his hands. "I don't understand what's happening. Why would someone want to take Melissa?" He looked up, eyes widening as a sudden thought struck him. "Do you think it might be her ex-husband? Did he track her down?" He struggled to rise to his feet. "We have to stop him. Melissa can't go back to him . . . She was so afraid . . ." Eddie reached out a hand, steadying him. "John, stop." He took in a deep breath, searching for the right words. "Melissa's not . . . She's not who you think she is." "What do you mean?"

With a sigh, Eddie pressed on, "There's no ex-husband, John. I told you that because her case was confidential—still is—but the truth is . . . The truth is someone is after her, trying to kill her. His name is R.W. Curran, and he's a paid assassin."

The name seemed to strike a chord with John, and his face paled. "The terrorist from the news? The one who killed Samantha?"

"Unfortunately, I can't say any more."

He forced himself to meet John's gaze full on, not flinching away as the shock in John's eyes melted into dismay, and then into anger. "All this time, you knew. You put my family in danger. You . . ." He shook his head. "Samantha died because of this, didn't she? And now Melissa's gone, probably—" He choked on the word. "—Probably dead." His eyes flooded with frustrated, helpless tears as he met John's gaze. "And you didn't even have the decency to warn me?"

Eddie swallowed. How to explain to John that the truth about Olivia was so much bigger than anything he could comprehend. How to explain that he'd felt he owed it to her, to have the chance to go someplace new where nobody knew who she was and what terrible burden she carried. How to explain that he'd made a promise to keep her safe and that he'd failed her time and time again, despite his best efforts? How does he explain how guilty he fells about Samantha's death?

But there were no words. "I'm sorry," he said instead, rising to his feet and leaving John alone to his grief.

Chapter Twenty-Eight

Flames. Coal. Ash. Olivia woke up, gagging, as the smell of a fireplace overwhelmed her senses, still recovering from the serum that had been injected into her. Everything was shrouded in darkness, a blindfold covering her eyes. She tried to move, but her wrists and ankles were bound—duct tape, from the feel of it.

Rolling over onto her side, she vomited.

Once the heaving and trembling had subsided, she became aware of two muffled voices coming from—where? Another room, it sounded like. Close by. She could scarcely make out any words, but from the lilt of the voices, she thought one must be Irish. One a man, the other a woman who spoke with a Middle Eastern accent, her voice low and gravelly, like she was a heavy smoker.

Why had they taken her? What were they going to do with her?

Stay calm, Olivia, she told herself, breathing in and out of her nostrils, deep and slow and controlled, though her heart was racing. *You'll find a way out. Stay sharp. Think.*

She heard a creak as the door to the room opened, and suddenly any efforts at calmness vanished, as she tensed, waiting for whatever might come. She heard slow, deliberate, heavy steps, and then suddenly a voice nears her ear—a man, gruff and strained.

"Scream all you like. But no one will hear you if you do."

The man lingered a minute longer, and Olivia waited for him to say something more. But then, abruptly, he turned and left, shutting the door behind him.

It was probably only five or so minutes that passed, but to Olivia, it felt like an hour. Then suddenly, the door was opening again, and a different set of footsteps crossed over to her—lighter, softer. A woman.

Once again, Olivia tensed, waiting. Feeling fabric pressed against her mouth, she instinctively jerked away, thinking it might be chloroform—or worse, that someone might be trying to smother her.

Then she realized that the person—the woman who'd been speaking with the man in the other room? —Was dabbing the side of her mouth, removing the vomit. She felt a bizarre impulse to say thank you for the unexpected kindness, but had to remind herself that she was being held here against her will, that she'd been injected with some kind of compound, dragged out of her hotel room . . .

And John. A sob nearly escaped her throat at the thought, but she bit it back. Was he searching for her? Worrying for her? Or had they left him dead, another casualty caused simply by being part of her world?

The ministrations of the towel stopped. She felt the rim of something plastic and cool press against her lips. "Drink this."

Olivia did as she was told. It was ginger ale, sweet and unexpected. She drained the entire glass, then waited to see if she would receive any further instruction, any clue of why she was here—any lifeline that she could clutch at. But without so much as another word, the woman stood and left the room.

Sometimes Olivia could pick up faint hints of a conversation coming from the other side of the wall. Though it was muffled, she could also hear it was one-sided—only the man's voice, gruff and angry.

"What do you mean, it was a mistake…? I already have her now… Then what am I supposed to do…?"

Minutes passed, stretching into hours. Olivia began to squirm on the rough cot as the ginger ale worked its way through her system. She had hoped someone else might come in to check on her, but no one did.

"Help!" she yelled out finally, her voice hoarse from lack of use. "I need to use the loo. Please, someone!"

It was more humiliating than she could describe, but still better than the alternative of wetting herself and having to simply lie in her own filth. For a few moments, she worried that might be their plan—a bizarre method of torture—but then she heard footsteps approaching. The woman.

She hustled around pulling something out from underneath the cot that clattered against the floor. Something metal? Then all at once she felt gruff fingers pulling up her dress, fishing around for her panties.

Olivia jerked away. "What are you doing?" "Said you had to wee," the woman reminded her. "Can't let you out, so you'll have to use the bed pan."

Tears of humiliation streaked down Olivia's blindfolded face. "Please. I won't try to run. Just let me use the toilet."

"Can't," the woman repeated, stubborn. "It's this or nothing."

A long moment of silence followed. "Fine." The woman's voice started to move away. "Suit yourself."

"Wait!" Olivia took in a sharp breath, steeling herself. "I'll use it. Please."

The woman shuffled back. A moment later, a humiliated Olivia maneuvered blindly over the cold metal pan. She had never been more mortified in her entire life, but she refused to let it show on her face. She would not give them the satisfaction of any more tears.

When she had finished, the woman helped arrange her thong and dress back into place before stepping back. "Don't you have anything to say to me?"

Olivia swallowed. "Thank you," she managed through gritted teeth.

Footsteps echoed across the floor, and the door slammed shut.

Chapter Twenty-Nine

An exhausted John returned to the Four Seasons after receiving the all clear from the hospital. First things first, he stopped in to check on Miles, who slept soundly, oblivious to everything that had taken place. "Everything all right?" John asked the sergeant, Andrea Ungretti, who'd been put in charge of watching Miles during his absence.

"Fine and dandy," Sergeant Ungretti returned. "You got a good kid here."

Despite the stress and heartache of the past 24 hours, John's face softened. "Yeah. I do." His only consolation in everything that had taken place was that Miles was still safe and sound, that no harm had come to him. Unlike—

Unable to even think her name without a wave of grief washing over him, John pressed a hand to his face to steady himself. When he looked up again, Sergeant Ungretti gave him a sympathetic smile. "Go get some sleep, Mr. Verner. I'll keep an eye on him."

A few hours of uninterrupted rest sounded like absolute heaven. Still, John shook his head. "No, that's all right. You've done enough already—"

"That's an order, Mr. Verner." Sergeant Ungretti's voice had a hard, no-nonsense edge to it, but her eyes were sympathetic.

Pretty lady, John mused to himself tiredly. He was surprised that Eddie hadn't made a move on her yet. His brother-in-law was a notorious playboy, though lately he'd dropped a few small hints that there might be somebody waiting for him at home. That was nice, John thought. Everybody needed somebody to come home to.

Melissa.

John sighed; this was a battle he would have to lose, it seemed. Not only was he exhausted, but he also felt like he was on the verge of tears at any given moment, and worry gnawed away at the pit of his stomach. A few hours' sleep might not change that altogether, but it could potentially take the edge off, at least a bit.

Finally, sighing, he relented. "Thanks. I owe you one."

Walking toward the adjoining bedroom, he paused, spotting Melissa's iPad. On sudden impulse, he tucked it underneath his arm, disappearing into the darkened chamber.

There was something important he was missing, something he was meant to know but couldn't quite place his finger on.

I'm not who you think I am— Melissa had been starting to tell him right before she disappeared. At the time, he thought she'd been alluding to the fact that she was in hiding from an abusive husband, but Eddie's recent revelations suggested something even darker, more dangerous.

Who are you, Melissa? He wondered to himself uneasily as he stared down at the tablet in his hands.

John half-heartedly skimmed through Melissa's iPad. Normally he would never resort to sneaking through someone's private things, but desperate times and all that; and besides, if it might help find her, he would gladly risk any anger she might have at his abuse of privacy.

However, it proved to be a moot point, since for all intents and purposes, Melissa's iPad was all but empty. She had no saved documents; all of her e-mails had been deleted; even her search history had been carefully and meticulously erased. If he hadn't seen her use it for himself time and time again, he would have believed that it was a brand-new machine. The only indications that the iPad actually belonged to somebody were a few purchased books—including *The Disappearance of Olivia.*

John frowned at the title. He'd read a few of the opening chapters and had been struck by some of the parallels to Melissa, despite some of the obvious, glaring differences—her coloring, for example, and the differences in names. But it was only a book . . . wasn't it?

Fighting his own exhaustion, John opened the document and picked up reading where he'd left off before. He was a quick reader, and it didn't take him long to make headway. Soon enough, his eye caught once again a familiar name:

Eddie Armstrong—inspector for Scotland Yard.

"Weird," John muttered to himself uneasily. He remembered reading that before, but somehow reading it again now after Eddie's slipup calling Melissa "Olivia," it stuck out even more. That couldn't be pure coincidence, could it?

He continued on, even more intently than before. It didn't take him long to reach the next pivotal plot points. That this Olivia Franklin was actually the biological daughter of Diana and Charles. That there were people who wanted to kill her for this information—who had killed her parents and countless others in pursuit. That she had been forced to go into hiding, to flee the country, to change her name . . .

The iPad slipped from his hands onto the bed. He was such an idiot. It all seemed too impossible and surreal to be true, and yet . . . it was so obvious at the same time.

Melissa Spencer wasn't Melissa Spencer at all. She was Olivia Franklin.

Chapter Thirty

An impatient Eddie paced the length of the Four Seasons lobby, mobile phone pressed to his ear. This was his third time trying to get ahold of Fred Connors, still with no reply. "Call me when you get this," he concluded briskly, snapping off his phone.

No sooner had he done so than the phone began to buzz. Eddie looked at it expectantly, anticipating Fred's name—but instead, it was John, calling him at five in the morning.

"This can't be good," Eddie muttered to himself, but obligingly took the call. "John? Have you heard something about Melissa?"

A long pause, and then John finally returned, "Don't you mean Olivia?"

Eddie sighed to himself. This wasn't going to pleasant. *"Bollocks."*

For a long time, Eddie and John merely stared each other down over their cups of coffee, delivered up to Verner's Four Season's suite. It was a conversation Eddie had always known would be inevitable, but somehow he had never prepared himself for how it should all begin.

Still, seeing as how John was glaring daggers at him across the table, silent and waiting, Eddie knew he'd have to be the one to plunge in. Taking in a deep breath, he did so. "So . . . sorry about hiding a fugitive princess in your house."

John merely blinked at him. "You think this is funny?"

Olivia, missing once again, Daniel dead, with a bullet between his eyes. No end in sight to all of this senseless violence and tragedy. No, not especially funny, but life had to go on somehow. Sighing, Eddie rubbed his face. "I think it was necessary, John. Her background was confidential, and it was my job to keep it that way."

"Bullshit," John hissed back at him. "You may not have been able to tell me the particulars, but you could have warned me that there were people after her, that taking her in was going to put my family at risk—"

They were interrupted as the door opened and Miles raced into the room, half-collapsing into his father's lap. "Dad! You've been gone forever." He glanced around, a small frown puckering his forehead. "Where's Melissa?"

Eddie and John exchanged a glance.

"Out shopping," John lied, forcing a smile for his son's benefit. "Why don't you go watch cartoons with Sergeant Andrea? I'll order some breakfast for you."

The excitement Miles had felt at the prospect of cartoons almost immediately faded at the mention of breakfast. "Not oatmeal?"

John laughed a little, despite himself. "Pancakes?"

"Okay!" And with that, Miles raced out of the room.

Eddie watched after him, shaking his head. "He sure loves Olivia."

John winced a little at the reference to her real name. "Yes, he does. And now she's yet another person in his life that I'm going to have to explain—"

Eddie didn't wait for him to finish, pressing on, "And she loves him. I've seen the way they are together. She loves that kid." He met John's gaze, and held it. "And she loves you, almost as much as you love her." He motioned to Olivia's iPad, sitting between them. "You read the book, so you know how much she's lost, what she's been through. Add to that the fact that she had to watch Daniel being murdered right in front of her very eyes, and you'll begin to get a picture of the kind of hell she's been through."

He let the words sink in shrugging. "Was it wrong to send her to you without giving you any warning? Maybe. Yes. But I knew you'd say no if you knew she came with any kind of danger, and I wanted to give her a chance. Maybe I had a hunch that you two would be exactly what she needed to put her back together again. She's been to hell and back, John. I just wanted to give her a little taste of heaven, too."

A moment of silence followed, John's face a blank stare. And then, he let out a deep, rueful sigh. "You're a manipulative bastard, you know that, Eddie?"

Eddie grinned back, just a little. "I know, but I'm not wrong."

A beat, then John abruptly averted his gaze, using a hand to shield his face. "Just bring her back to me, okay?"

Eddie swallowed. "I will."

Chapter Thirty-One

"Richard!"

Olivia awoke with a gasp, trying to detangle herself from whatever pinned her down. It took her sometime to remember she was bound hand and foot; another moment longer to remember the perpetual darkness was caused not only by the darkness of the room, but by the blindfold covering her eyes; and yet another minute to recognize the frantic, high-pitched sound of the woman's shouting, coming from the other room.

"Richard, wake up! Wake up!"

Abrupt silence followed, and then the door groaned in protest as it was thrown open, slamming against the wall. The woman's hands fumbled over Olivia's body, and she jerked away on instinct—until she realized the woman was cutting her free.

"Help him. You have to help him . . .!"

The blindfold was snatched from Olivia's eyes. She blinked at the sudden onslaught of light, and it took her a moment to adjust. Her gaze focused on the unfamiliar woman. She was heavyset, with a broad, flat face, looking to be in her fifties.

And in her hands, she held a gun, aimed directly between Olivia's eyes.

"Get up." The woman was trying to sound calm, but Olivia could hear the hysteria verging at the edge of her tone, the gleam of desperation in her eyes. "You have to help my husband."

Olivia nodded, clearing her throat to find her voice. "Take me to him."

The man, Richard, looked to be in his late fifties or early sixties. He was athletically built, tall—and his face was a disturbing gray pallor, so gray that it took Olivia a minute to recognize him as the man who had shot Samantha on the bridge. R.W. Curran, the man who had been hunting her for months. He lay sprawled on the couch, unconscious.

Despite everything these two had put her through, Olivia's medical training overtook any personal feelings she might have. She moved to Richard's side, feeling for his pulse.

As calmly as possible—so as not to incite any further alarm—Olivia met his wife's gaze. "Your husband is having a heart attack. I need you to help me get him to the floor so I can start CPR. Then I need you to call an ambulance."

The woman's eyes widened with panic, and she jerked her head. "They can't come here. He'll find out if they do . . ."

He? Olivia wondered to herself uneasily, but there was no time for that now. Still struggling to keep her voice calm, she motioned to Richard. "Help me get him to the ground."

Together, they managed to lower Richard to the ground. The woman hovered behind as Olivia felt for his pulse again and checked for any signs of breathing. None. She then checked his air passages, they were clear. Olivia began chest compressions.

It was a long, tiring, laborious process, but Olivia went at it mechanically, just as she'd been trained.

In the background, the woman paced, wringing her hands. "I told him to stop gambling, but sometimes I thought it was the only thing that gave him purpose anymore. They used him up in the air services and spit him out again, no thanks, no recognition. Then we get the call—one small thing, they said, but it wasn't small, not to Richard. We needed the money, but he needed to be a man again, too. I think that meant more to him than all the rest . . ."

Olivia ignored the speech as best she could, focusing on the task at hand. Finally, after three cycles of the process, Richard gasped a little, drawing in air. Relief surged through Olivia as color began to return almost immediately to his cheeks. She felt for his pulse again—faint, but present. Still, they would have to get him to hospital.

She glanced up at the woman, who had tears in her eyes as at the sign of renewed life. "He's okay now, isn't he?"

"For now." Olivia sat back, taking in a steadying breath. "But we need to get him to hospital because he is in serious condition."

The woman shook her head. "The closest hospital isn't for miles."

No sooner had Olivia begun to process this strange piece of information than the woman began pacing the room, twisting her hands together. "We can't let him know that Richard failed. He'll kill him."

A sharp dart of fear pricked Olivia's spine. Struggling to remain calm, she swallowed. "Who will kill him?"

"The man who hired him to kill you." The woman shook her head, still pacing. "I don't know who he was, but Richard called him 'Your Highness.'"

Olivia felt her mouth run dry, her breath catching in her throat. Someone from the Royal Family was trying to kill her? But who, and why? She'd stayed under the radar; she hadn't tried to draw any attention to herself. So why go through so much effort to silence her?

But those thoughts could wait. Yes, this man had been hired to kill her, had kidnapped her and held her for days . . . but she was a doctor. If she had the potential to save him, she had to do everything within her power.

"Listen to me very carefully," she told the woman, slowly so as not to incite panic. "If your husband isn't treated, he could die. I don't have the ability to know what triggered his attack. We need to get him to the nearest hospital as soon as possible. Do you understand?"

The woman hesitated for what felt like an eternity, and then nodded.

Olivia nodded back, briskly. "Good."

Together, they managed to carry Richard out to the rented Escalade that had brought Olivia to this dismal place. As soon as they had him situated in the backseat, Olivia felt for his pulse again to make certain he was still stable, then glanced up at his wife. "Do you have any aspirin?"

At the woman's nod of confirmation, Olivia continued, "Grab the bottle. It will help to stabilize him until we can get him to treatment. We have to get four pills into him."

She waited with Richard while the woman rushed inside. On impulse, she searched the car to see if the wife had been foolish enough to leave her car keys behind; there was no reason Olivia couldn't see that Richard got treatment on the way to turn him and his wife into the police. But the keys were missing in action, and she unfortunately hadn't watched enough American films yet to know how to hotwire a car, so she merely waited at Richard's side.

Shortly his wife reappeared, approaching the vehicle. "Good. Let's start him with two, early intervention can limit the damage and then we can see how he's progressing as we get closer to the hospital—"

Olivia glanced up and fell silent at the barrel of the gun now aimed in her face.

"No tricks, Princess," Curran's wife cautioned her. "Get into the front—you're driving." Then, shutting the door firmly on them, she moved to the passenger's side.

Olivia drove, hands clenched so tightly on the steering wheel that her knuckles had begun to turn white. She had absolutely no idea where she was. Outside of Florida and Boston, she knew next to nothing about maneuvering around in the states, not to mention driving in the snow and ice, and the woman in the passenger seat holding a gun to her temple didn't seem to be especially forthcoming with any information.

Seeing a button next to the rearview mirror for the OnStar help system, Olivia glanced over at the woman before slowly reaching for it.

Immediately, a woman's voice filled the car. "Hello, my name is Barbara. How can I be of assistance?"

Olivia swallowed, painfully aware of the cold metal pressing into her temple. *No tricks*, the woman had warned her, and despite her shaken state over her husband's health, Olivia had no doubt that she would use that gun.

"Hello, I'm a doctor with a man in my backseat who's had a heart attack. I need to get him to a hospital immediately, but don't know where the nearest one is."

She'd expected some hysterics from the other end, but Barbara either dealt with this sort of thing often, or she was a well-trained professional. "Just one second please. Okay . . . I'm reading here that the nearest hospital is 25 miles away."

Olivia calculated quickly. 25 miles—roughly half an hour or so. The roads were slick with snow so every minute might take three times as long.

After telling Barbara her plan, the woman was able to help her find her way to the main road. "I'll alert the highway patrol that you'll be heading down the I-93 South towards Littleton Regional Hospital."

"Thank you, Barbara." Olivia licked her lips, feeling a surge of unexpected bravery. Time to be a little daring, consequences be damned. "Can you tell me where I am, please?"

She was hoping that Richard's wife would be so preoccupied with worrying over her husband's health that she wouldn't notice the little slip-up, but she made a small whirring noise in her throat, glaring at Olivia over the barrel of the gun.

On the other end of the call, Barbara sounded confused. "You're on the I-93 South."

Receiving no response from Olivia, Barbara waited a beat before pressing on, "You mean in Franconia Notch, New Hampshire, correct?"

She still sounded confused, and for good reason. Why would a person have no idea what town, or even state, she was in?

Still painfully aware of the loaded gun aimed at her, Olivia swallowed, doing her best to keep her voice from shaking. "Yes."

With no other choice, she clicked off the call and just kept driving, eyes fastened firmly on the highway before her.

Chapter Thirty-Two

A knock on the hotel suite door interrupted Eddie mid-pace. He moved to answer it, revealing none other than Fred Connors. "Where the bloody hell have you been? I've been calling you all morning."

"Pouring over hours upon hours of security camera feed," Fred returned with a heavy yawn. "Haven't slept or eaten—thanks for asking."

Properly chagrined, Eddie pushed over the leftover pastries from his hasty breakfast with John earlier that morning. "Help yourself."

"Later." Without invitation, Fred opened Eddie's laptop, inserting his flash drive. "First, there's something I want to show you . . ."

Wordlessly, Eddie stepped into position beside him, watching as the images ran from the security feed began to play across the screen. He raised an eyebrow, impressed. "They let you take this for your own personal use?"

Fred shrugged. "I may or may not have spent a good portion of that time flirting with the hotel manager, a certain Ms. Malik." He glanced sidelong at Eddie. "Don't tell my wife."

"My lips are sealed."

All business once again, Fred motioned to the screen—a long corridor outside several rooms. "Okay, this is about 8:25 p.m. the night Olivia was abducted."

Eddie squinted at the numbers on the door. "And that's room 505, where Olivia was abducted from."

"Right. Watch this."

A stocky woman, who looked to be in her 50s, wearing a hotel uniform and pushing a cart, shuffled down the hall. She was such a nondescript figure that anyone watching the feed wouldn't have bothered to give her a second glance—if she hadn't paused just outside of room 502, glancing over both shoulders before reaching out to knock.

"Bingo," Eddie murmured.

Fred rubbed his chin. "Keep watching."

The door to room 505 opened, revealing John Verner. At almost the same moment, a second figure darted from the shadows—tall and sturdily built. As Fred and Eddie watched on, the man whipped something from behind his back—a nightstick, from the looks of it—and clubbed John over the head. The two pushed John backward into the room, closing the door behind them.

Eddie whistled low under his breath. Even knowing that John had emerged from the whole ordeal, it was still difficult to watch. "All right, but that still doesn't explain how they got Olivia out of the room with nobody noticing."

As if on cue, the feed jumped forward a bit. Fred motioned to the screen. "This is now about 8:40 that same evening. Watch."

The woman emerged from the room, followed by the man pushing what now seemed to be a significantly heavier, harder-to-maneuver cart.

"Holy hell." Eddie paused the screen, squinting in at the blurred image of the bellman. He met Freddie's face grimly. "That's R.W. Curran."

The next spliced fragment was taken from the curbside cameras. As Eddie and Fred watched on, R.W. Curran placed a body-sized bag—presumably, Olivia—into the back of a black Escalade. The woman shuffled over to the passenger side of the vehicle, while R.W. glanced over his shoulder before climbing behind the wheel.

Eddie once again paused the screen. "Take a look at those plates."

Fred did so. "A rental car. Good eye." He fished out his cell phone. "Which means it's probably equipped with an OnStar system."

Eddie felt a surge of hope flush through him. "Which means they'll be able to track the vehicle."

"Exactly."

A few calls later, Fred was put through to one of the operators named Barbara, who had apparently taken a strange call earlier that evening from a doctor with an British accent who had a heart-attack patient needing assistance getting to a hospital.

"The whole conversation seemed very strange," Barbara confided over speakerphone to the two men. "Something clearly wasn't right, but I attributed it to stress at the time. I was able to call in a police escort for them—they must have reached the hospital by now."

"And which hospital is that, luv?" Eddie inquired, pen and pad of paper at the ready.

"The Littleton Regional Hospital."

Another quick series of calls, and they were put through to the New Hampshire State Police. Fred explained the situation to them tersely and succinctly—that a British doctor was being held hostage, forced to help treat a heart attack victim en route to the Littleton Regional Hospital. After a few minutes of re-routing, they were put through to the squad car that had been assigned as escort.

"We left them at the hospital about fifteen minutes ago," Sergeant Randy Stone of the New Hampshire State Police department informed them. "Everyone made it inside safe and sound—the victim, a male in his late fifties, and two women, one in her fifties, the other in her early thirties. After making sure he'd been checked in, we left them there."

Eddie exchanged a glance with Fred. Olivia was a smart woman; there was no way she would have let those policemen leave without seeking help to escape—unless it would have put her in some kind of serious danger to do so.

"We need you to turn around and get back to that hospital as soon as possible," Fred instructed the sergeant. "The woman in her 30s—Melissa Spencer—is being held against her will, after an attempt on her life and a kidnapping by these same people. As quickly as you can—"

"We're already on our way," Sergeant Stone interrupted, followed by the sounds of shrieking sirens that blared through the phone's speaker.

Chapter Thirty-Three

The emergency room was organized chaos, people rushing about like mad to get from one place to the next. Olivia and Curran's wife watched on as a team of doctors and nurses worked on Richard—R.W. Curran, the man who'd been on her trail all this time.

As Olivia watched on, she felt something cold and hard press against her spine. The gun. Mrs. Curran's voice was harsh but unable to conceal her worry; her body angled in close enough that no one could see the concealed weapon. "Don't you dare try anything. Nothing's changed. As soon as they release him, we're going straight back, you hear?"

Olivia didn't respond, just gave a slight nod of her head—even as her mind was whirring, racing to find some way out of this.

Suddenly from outside came the screech of sirens—not entirely unusual for this place, with all the comings and goings of ambulances and other emergency vehicles. But this time it seemed much more concentrated, as if at least ten or so squad cars were approaching at once.

"What in the bloody hell?" Mrs. Curran asked nervously, glancing toward the nearby window.

Olivia didn't think, she just acted. As the triage team was working on Curran, Olivia swiped a scalpel from a trauma cart and concealed it in her sleeve before Mrs. Curran glanced back. "Come on. We're leaving, now. Richard's in good hands —"

Even as the words escaped her lips, all hell broke loose, the machines suddenly went wild as Richard began to code. All eyes were now on the emergency team and the man himself, including Mrs. Curran's. She gave a little gasp, releasing her pressure on the gun for a fraction of a second—but long enough for Olivia to whip behind her, holding the scalpel to her throat.

"Drop the gun," she hissed into the woman's ear.

One of the hospital staff glanced back, eyes widening at the sight. "What the hell is going on here?"

Just then, the doors burst open and a veritable army of police officers rushed into the room, weapons drawn and aimed. "Release your weapons!" the officer at point shouted.

Olivia tensed but waited until she heard Mrs. Curran's gun clatter to the floor before she, too, released her scalpel. In an instant, the officers swarmed in on them. "Melissa Spencer?" the first officer asked.

Tears flooded Olivia's eyes, and she managed a nod. Close enough, anyway. "Yes."

The officer—whose nametag read Sergeant Stone—offered her a kind smile. "From what I've heard, you've had a pretty rough couple of days. What do you say we get you back to Boston?"

Unable to stop the tears dripping down her cheeks, Olivia nonetheless did her best to smile, nodding. "I'd like that very much."

With all the attention focused on the commotion caused by Mrs. Curran's arrest and Olivia's rescue, it took very little effort for MI5 Special Agent Denise Feild to slip into R.W. Curran's room. His health was still touch and go, though the doctors had managed to stabilize him, at least for the time being.

Wasting no time, Agent Feild slipped a syringe out of her pocket and inserted the contents into Curran's drip feed. Digoxine. Combined with the medications already pumping through his system, even this mild overdose would prove to be deadly, but would be attributed to carelessness on the part of whoever distributed it, not any tampering from an outside source. It was the perfect crime.

Agent Feild wrapped up quickly and slipped out of the room just as the sounds of flatlining began to occur on the machines in Curran's room. She slipped easily into the throngs of other scrubbed medical professionals, veering toward an exit at the first opportunity and disappearing outside.

She didn't know what Curran had done to deserve being terminated, but that was not her concern. She'd merely happened to be at the right place at the right time when the order came, and she had followed through without questions and without complications. Her superior officer would be pleased.

Giving a small smile of grim satisfaction, Agent Feild punched in the code over her secure mobile phone to indicate success, then hailed the nearest taxi cab.

Receiving the message of confirmation from his contacts at MI5, Charles let out a sigh of relief. It was unfortunate that things with Curran had to end this way, but things had gotten entirely out of hand. Now nobody would be the wiser that he had ever been involved—including William and Harry.

Charles blanched at the thought. He would have to devise a way to silence Mrs. Curran as well. His sons—and the people of Britain—must never know what he had almost done.

He just hoped it was a secret Curran would take to his grave.

A loud knock on the hotel room door brought John to quick attention. He glanced over at Miles, who was napping at his side, before slipping out of the bedroom to answer it.

It was Eddie. John's breath caught in his throat, and he took a moment to compose himself before opening the door. Eddie glanced up, his face a perfect blank, impossible to read. Then, abruptly, he allowed the smallest of smiles.

"They found her, John. She's on her way back. Curran is dead and the woman he was with was his wife and she is in police custody."

Relief weakened John's knees, causing him to sag against the doorframe. He covered his face, and Eddie reached out to grasp his elbow, helping him to steady himself. John cleared his throat, struggling for composure. "Is she . . . did they hurt her?"

"Just a few bumps and bruises."

John took in several deep breaths, stabilizing himself both physically and mentally before he was once again able to meet Eddie's gaze. "Can I ask you a favor, Eddie?"

"Shoot."

"Can you not let her know yet—that I know who she is, and why she's here?"

John saw the confusion flash through Eddie's eyes, though he obligingly nodded. "Mum's the word."

A grateful John clapped his brother-in-law on the shoulder. "Thanks." He couldn't explain quite why it was so important to him that he should be the one to tell Melissa—*Olivia*, but it was. They needed a chance to clear the air between them, just the two of them.

And they would get it. Olivia was coming home to him. After thanking Eddie and asking him to keep him informed on any updates, John closed the door and sank down against it, burying his face against his hands.

Chapter Thirty-Four

They had some time to kill before Olivia's journey would end; it was a long drive from New Hampshire. After Miles woke up, John took him on a walk in the Boston Gardens.

The park was a veritable ice kingdom, full of beautiful ice-crested trees and bridges and gazebos—a decidedly different kind of beauty from Florida, of which Miles couldn't seem to get enough of. Finally the night before it had snowed, Miles was in heaven. He played in the snow as much as he was able, still wearing out quickly even though Madelina assured John he was well on the road to recovery. After a while, he fell into step with John, holding his gloved hand and babbling about everything he was going to tell Melissa once she got back from her shopping trip and speculating about what she might have bought him.

John was grateful that the boy remained oblivious to his silence, because if he'd been forced to speak at the moment he was sure he'd break down into tears at how close he'd come to having to explain to his son how yet another important person in his life wasn't coming back.

What a miracle that she was coming home to them. What a miracle it was to get a second chance.

When Miles really began to lag, John knew it was time to head back to the hotel. They cut through the now-familiar paths until they were back on the Boylston Street once more. As they began to cross the street at the corner of Arlington Street, John's phone began to buzz in his pocket. He waited until they were back on the sidewalk before answering, heart pounding with anticipation as he recognized Fred Connors's phone number.

It took him a couple tries to finally get out the word. "Hello?"

Fred, bless his soul, did not mince any words. "She's back."

Once Miles heard the news, John could not keep him from racing in the hotel toward the elevators—nor did he especially want to. He imagined if there was anyone more excited to see Melissa—*Olivia*—than his son, it was he. After everything that had happened, after everything he'd learned about her, he had to see her, face-to-face. To know if he could love Olivia Franklin the way he'd loved Melissa Spencer.

The elevator ride seemed painfully long, even though they were only going up four flights of stairs. Once the doors finally dinged open on the fourth floor, Miles was out like a shot, racing toward their suite and half-singing, half-chanting Melissa's name like some kind of mantra.

It was going to be confusing, trying to explain to Miles why they would have to start calling Melissa by another name. That was, if Olivia decided to stay with them at all.

The thought had never crossed John's mind before, and he paused mid-stride, a frown creasing his forehead. What if now that the cat was out of the bag, Olivia decided to move on to somewhere new? Somewhere she could disappear again? As much as he loved her, John honestly didn't know whether or not that would be for the best. He had never thought he could love another woman like he had Julia, but Olivia had nudged her way into his heart so gradually he'd scarcely realized it had happened until it was too late. The thought of being without her was like a knife to the chest—but at the same time, could he knowingly put his family in danger that way? If it were only himself, he wouldn't have questioned it. But could he do that to Miles?

They had finally reached the room. As Miles snatched the key card out of John's numb fingers and pushed open the door, John swallowed.

This was it. The moment of truth. Somehow, even without quite understanding why, he knew the second he saw her again, he would know what he had to do.

"Melissa!" Miles shrieked ahead of him, racing forward and disappearing around the corner.

Steeling himself, John turned.

Olivia was crouched down, holding Miles in her arms as silent tears streaked down her face. She looked tired, emotional, but otherwise no worse for the wear; at least she hadn't been hurt. John swallowed again as he looked at her. She was so beautiful.

"I missed you so much, sweetheart," she was whispering into Miles's ear. John must have made some noise as he approached, because she suddenly tensed and looked up; seeing him, her features softened once more. "Hi, John."

John released the breath he hadn't realized he'd been holding. He knew he should continue to cross the distance between them but felt frozen, his hands hanging awkwardly at his sides.

As if sensing his uneasiness, Olivia straightened, giving Miles's head one last affectionate pat before crossing the room to John. Tears streaming down her cheeks, she hesitated only a second before throwing herself into his arms.

John gripped her back just as fiercely, and in that moment, he knew. He would never let her go again—not ever.

An oblivious Miles approached, tugging on John's shirt. "Is it time for dinner yet?"

Fighting back his own tears, John managed a laugh. "Why don't you go look at the menu in the bedroom? You can turn on some cartoons while you wait."

Seeming overwhelmed by the double treat of in-room dining *and* television, a grinning Miles raced to the other room.

After he was gone, John pulled back to look Olivia in the eye. He could see, now, the almost artificial quality to the brown of her eyes, something he'd never noticed before. He wondered what she looked like as Olivia—the true Olivia. Either way, he knew he would love her as long as his heart still beat.

Giving her a tender smile, John cupped both sides of her face. "Welcome back . . . Olivia."

She started, her eyes darting back and forth between his as she searched for his reaction. But, seeing only kindness and acceptance there, she relaxed into a smile. "I wanted to tell you."

"I know." He hesitated before leaning forward and kissing her. It was a ghost of a kiss, light and chaste, and goodness knew he intended there to be a lot more where that came from. But first, they would have to get to know each other as John and Olivia. He could bide his time; she was worth the wait. "I could sure use a drink. You?"

Olivia broke into a grin. "You read my mind."

He crossed the room, pouring them both Bombay martinis before heading back, glasses in hand. "Would you like to make a toast?"

She smiled ruefully as she took the glass. "Why don't you do it? Being kidnapped always leaves me feeling terribly unclever."

John thought about it a moment before raising his glass. "To us, whoever we may be."

Olivia's eyes met his, and she smiled. "I'll drink to that."

Chapter Thirty-Five

Later that night, after Miles was asleep and in bed, Fred and Eddie joined them in the suite's living room for some well-earned drinks. Olivia hugged each man in turn, undyingly grateful for friends such as these who had put their lives on the line for her time and time again. Her parents would have been so happy to know she had ended up in such good hands.

And so would Daniel, Olivia mused, smiling as John reached out to take her hand. He had only ever wanted her to be happy. And somehow, despite everything that had happened, she was. Happier than she'd ever believed she could be again.

For a while, they all tried to avoid the topic, talk only of happier things. But finally when the silence stretched on too long, it was time to acknowledge what they'd all been trying to avoid—the secret that had united them and torn them apart and brought them back together again.

"There's a reason why I was so late joining you here in the States," Eddie informed Olivia, as he leaned back on the patio chair, nursing his gin and tonic. "I was doing a little follow-up investigation on Philip Churchill."

Olivia shivered automatically at the name. Seeing John's confusion, she elaborated, "The man who pieced together my true identity in the first place, killed my parents, and sent me on the run."

"Nice guy," Fred filled in dryly. "But what other leads could you dig up on him? He's been dead for over a year now."

Eddie nodded. "True. But I knew if we could get to the heart of why Churchill went off the rails the way he did, we could find the source behind the entire thing."

"The person who ordered the attack in the first place," Olivia breathed, mind flashing back. "While I was in her custody, Mrs. Curran mentioned something about the man her husband was working for. She said he'd referred to him as 'Your Highness.'"

The three men exchanged a significant glance. "That doesn't surprise me," Eddie spoke up. "In fact, it confirms what I found in my investigation . . ."

Eddie went on to describe what he'd uncovered in Churchill's personal diaries—including a line that had particularly stuck out to him. "'It's all about the bloody money!'" he quoted to them verbatim. "'Not succession, not anything but the money.'"

Olivia frowned, leaning forward. "But what could he mean by that . . .?"

"When you met William and Harry, you signed a document renouncing your claim to the throne—"

"That's right," Olivia interjected. It had never been about the money for her. She'd only wanted to meet her family.

"But the succession laws have changed." Eddie set down his glass, folding his hands together. "Even with that document, if news got out that there was another living heir—the rightful heir—can you imagine the media frenzy? But the throne isn't all that's at stake."

Realization dawned on Olivia. "It's all about the bloody money."

Fred glanced back and forth between them, confused. "I don't get it. I'm no expert on British monarchy by any stretch of the imagination, but I thought the grounds and the Crown Jewels and whatnot all belonged to the people now?"

Eddie looked impressed, despite himself. "So what, Americans can read now?"

Fred managed a wry grin. "There was a YouTube video about it."

Shaking his head, Eddie looked back to Olivia. "Our Yank friend is right, but less commonly known is that a vast amount of personal wealth is conveyed to the sitting monarch."

"'Vast amount'?" Olivia echoed faintly.

Eddie shrugged. "Somewhere in the area of one billion dollars."

Beside Olivia, John coughed into his drink. "Well," he managed once he'd recovered himself, "at least we know you're not after my money."

"I guess with that much money at stake, we won't be seeing the end to people trying dispose of Olivia out of the way anytime soon," Fred mused.

A silence fell over the group, all traces of good humor vanished. John was the first to speak, his grip iron-tight on Olivia's hand. "So what do we do?"

"Someplace new would be our safest bet." Eddie leaned back, folding his arms over his chest. "If R.W. Curran traced you here, someone else will, too. How do you feel about Canada?" Olivia we still don't know who hired Churchill and Curran, and with both of them dead we will probably never know."

"No," Olivia spoke up, firmly.

Eddie grimaced in understanding. "I feel the same way—far too much hockey for my taste—but it might be our best option . . ."

"No," Olivia said again. "I'm not going to hide anymore." Casting a quick glance at John, she pressed on, "It's time to tell the world who I really am. The only way to protect myself and the people I love is not to give anyone a reason to try to silence me before the word gets out— because the word will already *be* out."

Another silence fell, but this time more speculative. After a moment, Eddie nodded. "You do realize that you're going to become the most famous person on the planet."

"Bigger than Bieber?" Fred quipped.

"Bigger than Bieber," Eddie confirmed, shaking his head. "But maybe it's for the best. If everyone knows who you are and every eye is on you, that means no one can do you any harm without the entire eye of the world turning in on them, too."

Olivia released a deep sigh, pleased. "So, it's settled then. As soon as I get back to Palm Beach, I'm making an announcement to the press."

Fred grinned, leaning forward on the table. "I think I know some-one who might be able to help you with that . . ."

Once the team at Cosmo & Co. had finished with Olivia, she looked at herself in the mirror. She was thrilled. In anticipation of the story about to be released, Olivia booked a total spa day. Helen, a British expatri-ate and genius colorist had returned Olivia's hair back to its original blonde. The only thing left was to remove her brown contact lenses.

She'd spent so long pretending to be Melissa Spencer that for a moment, the woman in the reflection looked like a stranger; but then, adjusting, Olivia's eyes welled with tears as she realized she'd never have to pretend to be anyone else, ever again.

"It's perfect." She smiled warmly at the team who had worked so hard to restore her to herself. "Thank you."

She was ushered into a studio at WPTV where in a few minutes the interview would take place. Before she had time to marvel about the space and the cameras, her eyes fell on Luke Connors, a.k.a. Luke Detroit, and she broke into a broad grin. In all the madness of every-thing going on, this was the first time she'd actually had a chance to see him face-to-face after all these years.

Luke's grin mirrored her own as he crossed the room to her and engulfed her in a giant hug. In so many ways, he resembled Fred, but she couldn't help but note the marked differences, too—namely, his bright blonde hair, white-white teeth, and deep, deep tan.

"It's so good to see you, Princess!" he murmured as they broke apart.

"You, too," Olivia returned sincerely, and couldn't help but add, "You look like a cheesy puff."

Luke just laughed. "But a very well-paid cheesy puff." "I should hope so."

Still smiling, he took her hand, giving it a reassuring squeeze. "Are you ready for this?"

Taking in a deep breath, Olivia steeled herself. "As ready as I'll ever be."

Epilogue

Olivia stood at the bough of the *Julia*, allowing the warm spring air to whip through her blonde hair. It had been a little over three weeks since the airing of her 'outing' as a princess on the news, and as predicted, the media frenzy had been terrible. Only the support from good friends like Eddie, Fred, Luke, encrypted e-mails from Harry, William, and Kate, with attached photos of nephew Prince George and niece Princess Charlotte, and of course, having John and Miles by her side, had enabled her to get through the mayhem.

So far, no official statement had been released from Buckingham Palace, and she still hadn't received any acknowledgment from Charles. There were plenty of people who thought she was a fraud, a schemer, and a gold-digger, while others were desperate to get as close to the newest "princess" as they could. She was both one of the most hated and most loved women in the entire world—something she imagined her birth mother had known a thing or two about. Olivia wished more than anything now that Diana was here so that she could ask for her advice, on this and so many other things

But it had been worth it, admitting to the world who she was, Olivia thought to herself privately as she stared at the disappearing shoreline. They would be safe now, forever.

A hand slipped around her waist, platinum ring glinting in the sunlight. "Ready for a new adventure, Mrs. Verner?" John murmured into her ear.

Olivia smiled, leaning back against him and tilting her face up so she could see him. "With you, Mr. Verner?" She kissed him, full and deep. "I'd go anywhere."

From inside the cabin came Miles's delighted giggles. Glancing back, Olivia and John both laughed at the sight of him attempting to steer the yacht, guided by their on-deck captain.

Watching Miles, with John's arms wrapped around her, Olivia couldn't remember having ever been happier. Whatever life threw her way now, she was ready.

It was going to be a brilliant adventure.